GOODBYE MY PRECIOUS CHILD

DI SALLY PARKER #6

M A COMLEY

JEAMEL PUBLISHING LIMITED

GOODBYE MY PRECIOUS CHILD

DI SALLY PARKER #6

M A COMLEY

New York Times and USA Today bestselling author M A Comley
Published by Jeamel Publishing limited
Copyright © 2019 M A Comley
Digital Edition, License Notes

All rights reserved. This book or any portion thereof may not be reproduced, stored in a retrieval system, transmitted in any form or by any means electronic or mechanical, including photocopying, or used in any manner whatsoever without the express written permission of the author, except for the use of brief quotations in a book review or scholarly journal.

This is a work of fiction. Names, characters, places and incidents are a product of the author's imagination or are used fictitiously, and any resemblance to actual persons living or dead, business establishments, events or locales is entirely coincidental.

OTHER BOOKS BY M A COMLEY

Blind Justice (Novella)

Cruel Justice (Book #1)

Mortal Justice (Novella)

Impeding Justice (Book #2)

Final Justice (Book #3)

Foul Justice (Book #4)

Guaranteed Justice (Book #5)

Ultimate Justice (Book #6)

Virtual Justice (Book #7)

Hostile Justice (Book #8)

Tortured Justice (Book #9)

Rough Justice (Book #10)

Dubious Justice (Book #11)

Calculated Justice (Book #12)

Twisted Justice (Book #13)

Justice at Christmas (Short Story)

Justice at Christmas 2 (novella)

Justice at Christmas 3 (novella)

Prime Justice (Book #14)

Heroic Justice (Book #15)

Shameful Justice (Book #16)

Immoral Justice (Book #17)

Toxic Justice (Book #18)

Overdue Justice (Book #19)

Unfair Justice (a 10,000 word short story)

Irrational Justice (a 10,000 word short story)

Seeking Justice (a 15,000 word novella)

Caring For Justice (a 24,000 word novella)

Savage Justice (a 17,000 word novella Featuring THE UNICORN)

Gone In Seconds (Justice Again series #1)

Ultimate Dilemma (Justice Again series #2)

Shot of Silence (Justice Again #3)

Taste of Fury (Justice Again #4)

Crying Shame (Justice Again #5)

To Die For (DI Sam Cobbs #1) Coming Dec 2021

To Silence Them (DI Sam Cobbs #2) Coming Jan 2022

Clever Deception (co-written by Linda S Prather)

Tragic Deception (co-written by Linda S Prather)

Sinful Deception (co-written by Linda S Prather)

Forever Watching You (DI Miranda Carr thriller)

Wrong Place (DI Sally Parker thriller #1)

No Hiding Place (DI Sally Parker thriller #2)

Cold Case (DI Sally Parker thriller#3)

Deadly Encounter (DI Sally Parker thriller #4)

Lost Innocence (DI Sally Parker thriller #5)

Goodbye, My Precious Child (DI Sally Parker #6)

The Missing Wife (Coming Feb 2022)

Web of Deceit (DI Sally Parker Novella with Tara Lyons)

The Missing Children (DI Kayli Bright #1)

Killer On The Run (DI Kayli Bright #2)

Hidden Agenda (DI Kayli Bright #3)

Murderous Betrayal (Kayli Bright #4)

Dying Breath (Kayli Bright #5)
Taken (Kayli Bright #6 coming March 2020)
The Hostage Takers (DI Kayli Bright Novella)
No Right to Kill (DI Sara Ramsey #1)
Killer Blow (DI Sara Ramsey #2)
The Dead Can't Speak (DI Sara Ramsey #3)
Deluded (DI Sara Ramsey #4)
The Murder Pact (DI Sara Ramsey #5)
Twisted Revenge (DI Sara Ramsey #6)
The Lies She Told (DI Sara Ramsey #7)
For The Love Of… (DI Sara Ramsey #8)
Run For Your Life (DI Sara Ramsey #9)
Cold Mercy (DI Sara Ramsey #10)
Sign of Evil (DI Sara Ramsey #11)
Indefensible (DI Sara Ramsey #12)
Locked Away (DI Sara Ramsey #13)
I Can See You (DI Sara Ramsey #14)
I Know The Truth (A psychological thriller)
She's Gone (A psychological thriller)
The Caller (co-written with Tara Lyons)
Evil In Disguise – a novel based on True events
Deadly Act (Hero series novella)
Torn Apart (Hero series #1)
End Result (Hero series #2)
In Plain Sight (Hero Series #3)
Double Jeopardy (Hero Series #4)
Criminal Actions (Hero Series #5)
Regrets Mean Nothing (Hero #6)

Prowlers (Hero #7)

Sole Intention (Intention series #1)

Grave Intention (Intention series #2)

Devious Intention (Intention #3)

Merry Widow (A Lorne Simpkins short story)

It's A Dog's Life (A Lorne Simpkins short story)

Cozy Mystery Series

Murder at the Wedding

Murder at the Hotel

Murder by the Sea

Death on the Coast

Death By Association

A Time To Heal (A Sweet Romance)

A Time For Change (A Sweet Romance)

High Spirits

The Temptation series (Romantic Suspense/New Adult Novellas)

Past Temptation

Lost Temptation

ACKNOWLEDGMENTS

Thank you as always to my rock, Jean, I'd be lost without you in my life.

Special thanks as always go to @studioenp for their superb cover design expertise.

My heartfelt thanks go to my wonderful editor Emmy Ellis, my proofreaders Joseph, Barbara and Jacqueline for spotting all the lingering nits.

A special shoutout to all the wonderful Bloggers and Facebook groups for their never-ending support of my work.

To Mary, gone, but never forgotten. I hope you found the peace you were searching for my dear friend.

PROLOGUE

July 2000

The two children giggled excitedly. Anna's heart swelled with love and joy for the first time in ages. No, that wasn't quite true. When she was with her adorable children she was frequently at peace and happy—it was the other things in her daily existence that she had a hard time dealing with. Life as a single parent not only stretched the realms of capabilities but also the purse strings. She'd saved up for a few weeks for the bus fare alone to take the children to the Great Yarmouth Marina leisure park. They deserved a treat; they were good kids. Actually, they deserved much more than just a day trip out to have some fun. She was doing everything she was capable of to change that. She'd started a new job just over a month before, which meant that payday had arrived at the end of the previous week. This was her first real opportunity to spoil her wonderful kids, apart from the extra chocolate bar she'd bought them in the weekly shopping which she intended sharing with them the following day.

That night, however, she had something selfish to look forward to: her first date in five years. Dean was a colleague. He worked in the office next to hers. He was a high-flyer in the business, according to the secretary, Cynthia, working alongside her. Anna couldn't believe her luck when Dean took time out of his busy schedule to chat with her every chance he could.

Cynthia had giggled. "Looks like our Dean has a crush on you, young lady."

Anna was gobsmacked. After years of being single, the thought that a man—a handsome, wealthy one at that—would find her attractive had her heart fluttering every time he breezed past her desk, which was becoming more and more frequent. He'd finally plucked up the courage to ask her out on a date. Hence the reason she'd brought the children out that day, maybe to ease her guilt at leaving them for the first time in years. She was a constant in their lives. There when they woke up, came home from school, and when it was time to put them to bed at night. This date meant everyone's routine was about to be disrupted. She hoped wearing them out at the leisure centre would help them all make the transition without too many hitches.

"Mum, can Millie and I go down the slide? I'll watch her, she'll be safe, I promise."

Anna smiled at Louie. He was twelve, older than his sister, Millie, who was only six. Their father had been put in prison years before. She'd lost contact with him since then. They had never married; he'd never really wanted the kids. He used to beat Anna up at every chance, but the second he had struck Louie, that had been it. She'd packed up what little possessions they'd had and left the house. She'd contemplated going back home to her parents in London but had decided against it at the last minute, knowing how domineering her mother could be regarding the children's upbringing. She drove Anna nuts. So she'd ended up in a hostel for a few months until she'd found a job in a shop. The kindly manageress had felt sorry for her and offered her the flat above as temporary accommodation.

Anna had sourced all her furniture on her meagre wages from the nearby charity shop. The children were a credit to her, never pestering her for money she didn't have. They were aware she did her best for them, often putting their needs ahead of her own. She always ensured their bellies were full before she sat down to eat her own paltry meals.

She reflected on her past and shuddered. She'd come a long way in such a short time and only had herself to thank for the lovely flat they now lived in. Some of the furniture had been replaced and was being paid for on zero percent finance deals that she was setting money aside for. Her life was getting increasingly better with each passing month. Her new job was the icing on the cake, and her date with Dean was the cherry on top of that.

She watched the children playing with each other. Despite the difference in ages, Louie was his younger sister's guardian angel, watching her every move, especially when they got out of their depth in the water. He'd secured the armbands on Millie. Anna looked on from her lounger as she read her classic novel *Gone with the Wind*. Another hour or so, and the kids would be like shrivelled prunes; they'd need to go home then. She hated to spoil their fun, but now she was earning a regular income, she felt confident that trips like this would be a regular occurrence in their future.

"Mum...over here. Look at us." Louie waved from the top of the slide, his sister already in position for the descent. He positioned one leg on either side of Millie, and they both waved their arms in the air during their journey.

Anna's heart was in her mouth when they got near the bottom. They both hit the water, and Louie swiftly swam to his sister's side. Millie was coughing and spluttering, but being in her brother's arms made her laugh out loud and shout, "Do it again, Louie."

So they got out of the water and ran to the slide once again. This went on for the next half an hour. Anna glanced at her watch; time was getting on now. As much as she hated spoiling their fun, it was time to get ready and go. The bus was due in twenty minutes. "Louie, Millie, make this the last slide now. We need to go soon."

"Aww...Mum," Louie complained, his smile slipping as he reached for his sister's hand.

"Can't we stay, Mum, pwease?" Millie added, egged on by her older brother.

"I promise we'll come back next week, how's that?"

Louie trudged over to the slide, whispered something in his sister's ear, and together they ascended the steps.

Anna got the children's clothes ready to take into the changing rooms, then she bundled all their belongings into the bags. She glanced up to see the children laughing and screaming as they came down the slide for the final time.

"Come on, you two terrors. Out you come." She held a towel open for Millie and then a second one for Louie.

"We had the best time ever, Mum. Thanks for bringing us here today." Louie smiled and pecked her on the cheek.

"You're welcome. I wish I had the money to bring you here more often. Who knows what the future might have in store for us all? Let's get you two changed. We've got ten minutes before the bus arrives."

They rushed into the changing rooms. Louie went into the boys' while Anna took Millie's hand and led her into the girls'. They met up again five minutes later and ran to the bus stop together, giggling.

Once the bus arrived and they were settled in their seats, Anna presented each of them with a small bag of nuts to replace the energy they had burnt off.

Her thoughts turned to what she should wear for her date with Dean. Did she go casual? Or should she wear the one decent dress she owned?

She was still trying to decide a few hours later, after she'd made the kids pasta, baked beans and cheese, one of their favourite meals, and the babysitter, Lisa, had arrived. Lisa had been visiting them on and off for a few weeks now, to get her used to the children before she babysat them. She was the teenage daughter of one of the ladies at work who was delighted that Anna was going on her first date in years. She'd volunteered her daughter's services. Lisa was a dab hand at dealing with younger children and wanted to be a nanny when she was a little older.

She took Lisa into the bedroom and pointed at the outfits she'd spread out on the bed. "First date, which one should I choose?"

Lisa rubbed at her chin with her thumb and forefinger. "I would go the casual route—the trousers and sparkly top if I were you. The dress is pretty, though," she added quickly as if not to cause offence.

Anna laughed. "Trousers it is then. Thanks, Lisa. I'll have a quick shower and be out in a few minutes. The kids are watching *Toy Story*. That should keep them amused for a while."

"I've brought an assignment with me. I need to crack on with it over the weekend. It's due on Tuesday, and I'm only a third of the way through it."

"Assignment, for college? What subject?"

"The history of the lightbulb." She rolled her eyes.

"Oh goodness me, that can't be right, surely? Fancy the teacher marking all the papers. They're bound to say the same thing, aren't they?"

"That's where the problem lies. We've got to use our imagination and come up with something unique to say about them."

"Will Google help?"

Lisa sighed. "I'm hoping so. Enough about my woes, you get yourself ready. What time do you want the children in bed by?"

"Millie no later than seven, just after I leave in fact, and Louie, hopefully, will be exhausted from his adventures today. Make it nine for him, although I suspect he'll go much earlier, knowing him. He's never really been one for staying up late. They share a room. He's really considerate and won't wake Millie. Once she's asleep, you shouldn't hear a peep out of her."

"They're a credit to you, Mrs Pickrel."

"Please, call me Anna. Thank you; they truly are the greatest kids ever to grace this earth."

"I'll leave you to get ready; your date will be here soon. Are you excited or nervous?"

"A bit of both. Am I allowed to say that?"

"Understandable. You'll enjoy yourself, I'm sure."

"I hope so. The trouble is, everything has revolved around the kids for so long I'm not sure how I'm going to converse with an adult."

"Nonsense, you'll be fine. Mum says you've slotted in well at work. She likes you anyway. Oops, should I have said that?"

They both laughed.

"I'm glad. I like your mum, too."

Lisa smiled and left the bedroom. Anna jumped in the shower, dried her hair then swiftly pulled on her black trousers and sparkly silver top and studied her reflection in the mirror. She nodded her approval and went back into the bathroom to apply her makeup. She had decided to keep it subtle for this evening. She wouldn't want to give Dean the wrong impression. She gasped when the doorbell rang. Terror struck her heart and glued her to the spot.

Lisa knocked on the bedroom door a few seconds later. "Anna, your date has arrived."

"Thanks, Lisa. I'll be right out." One last study of her reflection, and she was satisfied by the overall effect. She left the bathroom and slipped into the one pair of decent shoes she possessed, the ones she wore to work every day, hoping to disguise them under her trousers in case Dean noticed them.

She emerged from the bedroom to find Dean chatting to the children in the lounge. Again, her heart clattered against her ribs. Dean was aware she had children; she hadn't wanted to mislead him in any way. He'd told her that he had a younger brother he was really fond of and her having kids didn't bother him in the slightest.

"Wow, you look amazing," Dean praised, the moment he laid eyes on her.

Her cheeks heated. "Gosh, thank you. I hope the children have made you feel welcome?"

"They have. I fear I've interrupted their movie. Louie was just telling me about your adventures today. Sounds like you all had a fabulous time."

"You'll have to come with us one day, Dean," Louie shouted, excitedly.

"I'd love to. If your mum would be up for that." He turned to look at her, his pearly white teeth sparkling under the living room light overhead.

"We'll see. Are you ready?" She was anxious to leave. Wanted time alone with him in case either of the children said something unfavourable before she had a chance to really get to know him.

"Okay, I'm all yours for the evening. Nice to meet you, Millie and

Louie. You, too, Lisa. Give us a shout if there are any problems, and we'll come straight home."

Anna smiled, appreciating his thoughtfulness. "Thank you, that means a lot."

The kids bid them an eager farewell and rushed over to the bay window ready to wave them off. Anna laughed and blew them kisses from the doorway.

"Be good for Lisa."

"We will," Louie called out.

Dean was the perfect gentleman. He opened the door to his sporty Audi, and she relaxed instantly into the front seat.

"Where are we going?" she asked, not giving him a chance to insert the key in the ignition.

"You'll see when we get there. I suppose I should have asked if there was any type of food you can't eat before I made the reservation."

"Shellfish, that's about all."

"Good. I think we'll be safe this evening then. I'll bear it in mind for future dates."

She was dumbstruck. How did she respond to that when this date hadn't even begun?

"Your kids... Do you mind me calling them that?"

"No, not at all. What about them?"

"They're wonderful. Well-behaved, you're an excellent mum."

"I'm not saying it's been easy, but we've survived admirably over the years. They appreciate the little things in life. Know there isn't a lot of money for us to spend on days out et cetera. So when they go out, they make sure they have a good time. Have you ever wanted kids? Sorry, that was a stupid question so early on in the date."

"No, it wasn't. One day I'd love to settle down and have kids of my own."

"Just not other people's kids," Anna mumbled her response.

"Now you're putting words into my mouth. I didn't say that."

"Sorry. Let's talk about something else instead."

"Like what?"

Anna pulled a face. "Heck, I don't know."

They both laughed. Dean drove for another twenty-five minutes and then pulled up outside a posh-looking Italian restaurant.

"Yummy, I love pasta."

"Good, this place is the top Italian restaurant in the area."

"Oh my, you didn't have to do this."

"Don't be silly. I wanted our first date to be a memorable one."

There he goes again, our first date, as if he's already intending on asking me out on another one.

Once they'd left the car, he hooked her hand through his arm and led her into the restaurant. "I have a table booked for Dean Sutton."

"Ah, yes, good evening again, Mr Sutton. If you'd care to wait over there for a moment, I'll see if your regular table is ready for you," the little man said. He bowed slightly and backed away from them.

"Thank you. Shall we?" Dean motioned for Anna to take a seat.

The maitre d' promptly appeared again. "Your table is ready now if you'd care to follow me."

The restaurant was quite empty. Anna assumed it would get busier as the evening progressed. The maitre d' held the chair out for her and tucked it under her legs once she was ready.

"Can I get you some drinks?" he asked.

"I'll have a sweet white wine if you have one," Anna replied, offering the attentive man a smile.

"I'll have half a lager as I'm driving, thanks, Luigi."

The man bowed again and left the table.

"Oh no, I forgot about that. I could have called a taxi and met you here."

"It's no problem. What do you fancy to eat?" Dean handed her a menu.

Not having been in a restaurant for years, she was out of her depth, even more so when she read the menu and found it was written in Italian. She glanced up to find him staring at her. "I don't know any Italian. You'll have to choose for me."

"Okay, what type of things do you like? Steak, chicken, bolognaise? Don't tell me you're one of these women who is constantly watching their weight."

"I'm not. I mean, yes, I do, but I don't let it rule my life. What do you recommend?"

"I love pasta and tend to stick with that."

"I'll have what you're having. Anything is fine by me as long as…"

"It doesn't have any shellfish in it, right?"

She giggled. "Glad to see you were listening."

"I was."

He ordered the meal, and they chatted generally until the main course arrived. Dean had decided to skip the starters as he said the portions were on the generous side and didn't want to overwhelm her.

He wasn't wrong either. When it arrived, Anna's meal was huge. Pasta bolognaise with a portion of garlic bread. "I'll never eat all this. Crikey, I could feed myself and the kids on this for a whole week."

He roared with laughter. "A slight exaggeration on your part, I think. Eat what you can."

Anna's mobile rang halfway through the meal and her home number popped up on the screen. "Sorry, it's home, I have to get it."

"Of course. Be my guest."

"Hello."

"Anna, I'm so sorry to disturb you. Oh God, I don't know what to do…"

"Lisa, calm down. What's wrong?" Her heart raced as she stared at Dean.

His brow was wrinkled with concern.

"It's my dad. He's had a heart attack. I need to get to the hospital, Mum needs me."

"Oh God, I'm sorry to hear that. Of course you must go. I'll come back to the flat now."

"Okay, I'm so sorry to spoil your evening. The kids are both in bed."

"It's all right. You go, I'll be there within thirty minutes. Make sure the door is locked behind you. Let me know how your father is when you get the chance." *Damn why had they come this far for a meal?*

"I will. If you're sure you don't mind?"

"I'm sure." Anna ended the call. "I have to go. I'm so sorry to spoil the evening like this. Lisa's father has had a heart attack."

"Damn, it's no problem. I'll settle the bill and take you home."

"Are you sure? God, I hate to do this, but there's no way I can leave the kids alone."

He raised a hand to prevent her saying anything else. "No need to apologise. Let's go."

Twenty minutes later, they arrived back at the flat to find an ambulance outside, its emergency lights rotating, lighting up the close where they lived.

"Oh God. No…" Anna ran into the flat. "Louie, Millie, what's going on?" She barged into the bedroom to find Louie standing at the end of his sister's bed while two paramedics were on either side of it. One of them was performing CPR on Millie.

"No! What's wrong with her?"

The other paramedic rushed to be with her. "Louie called nine-nine-nine and said that an intruder got into the house and…well, Millie was suffocated. We're doing our best to revive her now. I have to prepare you for the worst."

Anna glanced at her son. Tears streamed down his face. She reached out her arms, and he ran into them.

"I'm sorry, Mum. I went to the bathroom and when I came back a man was standing over her, pressing down on the pillow. I shouted at him and chased him. I rang nine-nine-nine like you told me to. She's gone, Mum."

Millie is gone…

The paramedic stepped away from the bed and shook his head.

Anna dropped to her knees and let out a spine-chilling scream, followed by, "My baby is dead."

1

"You'll sit down and eat a wholesome breakfast before you set off for work, Wifey."

Sally Parker shook her head at her new husband. "I've heard about newlyweds piling on the pounds. I'd rather not if it's all the same to you. A yoghurt will do for me. It's far too hot for anything else anyway."

"Trust me. You'll enjoy what I've knocked up. Sit down and stop complaining."

Sally glanced up at the clock on the wall. It was telling her that if she didn't leave in fifteen minutes, she would be late for work. If that happened, she'd feel out of sorts for the rest of the day.

"Sit," he ordered a second time.

She huffed out a frustrated breath. He turned back to the food he was preparing and flicked the switch on the kettle.

"At least let me make the coffee. I feel useless sitting here like a spare part."

"My kitchen, my rules." He peered over his shoulder and grinned then he poured the boiling water into two mugs and stirred them.

Sally picked up an unopened letter from the centre of the table. "When did this arrive?"

"Sorry, I forgot to tell you. Yesterday."

"It's from the bank, confirming my account has changed to my new name."

"Excellent news. One chore down, only dozens to go." He deposited a bowl of fresh fruit, topped with Greek yoghurt and a drizzle of honey, in front of her along with a mug of instant coffee.

"Wow, this looks amazing. It must have taken you ages to prepare," she replied, ignoring what he'd mentioned about the chore she had deliberately placed to one side. Did it really matter that she wasn't in the right frame of mind to alter her name just yet? Yes, she was dying to get rid of her ex-husband's name, but the thought of changing everything over was a truly daunting task she couldn't cope with right now. She had every intention of doing it in the near future in her personal life but had decided it would be better to keep things as they were for work—less complicated that way. Simon had made his feelings known about that in the past few days, which had led to their first marital tiff. This was his way of making it up to her.

"You're worth the effort. Our marriage is worth the effort. I'm sorry for shouting off my mouth last night. It's your decision, and I shouldn't try and dissuade you otherwise."

"As I already told you, I'll change everything personal. I just think it'll be better if I stick with Parker at work, at least for now."

He prevented her from taking her first mouthful of breakfast with a kiss on the lips. "Ignore me. You're your own person, Sally. I'll never force you to do anything against your will, I promise you." He sat in the chair next to her.

She placed a hand over his. "I know you won't. Honestly, I'm dying to get rid of Darryl's name at the earliest opportunity, but it'll simply be easier for me to remain Parker at work."

"I know." He tucked into his mango and pineapple. "What's on your agenda today?"

"The usual, looking through the rest of the cold case files and deciding which one to delve into next. I think there are still over forty-odd cases for us to investigate which that confounded Falkirk messed up."

Goodbye My Precious child

"Damn, I don't envy you one iota. Want to hear what I'll be up to?"

"Of course. This is wonderful by the way." She smiled and ate a few stoned cherries along with the yoghurt.

"Your dad and I are off to the auction house to see if there are any bargains to be had."

"What? Have you finished renovating all the other houses in your portfolio yet?"

"Almost. Your dad is brilliant at calling in favours from his mates. He's amazing, I love working with him. He's so knowledgeable about the houses in this area. Especially with the background needed about the relevant builders. Anyway, I don't want to bore you with the finer details of the business."

"Nonsense, I'm interested. Have you decided whether to give up your job yet?"

Over the past few months, Simon had become dissatisfied with his role as the area's one and only pathologist of any note. He sighed and took a sip of his coffee. "Still undecided, erring on the side of giving it up in favour of working with your father full-time. He's a fabulous man, but then, you already know that, right?"

"Yeah, he's pretty cool. Do you think the dynamics would change if you two were together constantly? Or is that me overthinking things?"

"I don't know. We all need to sit down and have a good chat about the future, I think."

Sally glanced up at the clock again. She rushed down the last few spoonfuls of her breakfast and dropped the bowl in the sink then drained her cup. "I've gotta fly."

"Go. I'll clear up. I'll fling the dirties in the dishwasher, don't worry."

She kissed him and gave him a hug. "You're amazing. Thank you for being you. Don't ever change."

He caught her by the wrist and looked her in the eye. "I won't, I promise. You're safe with me, never forget that."

"I know. Thank you."

He left his half-eaten breakfast and walked her out to her car where he kissed her again and hugged her tightly. She felt secure in his arms. Something she'd never felt in Darryl's. If he'd ever laid hands on her, it was during sex or when he wanted to control her. She shuddered at the thought of what she'd allowed him to put her through.

"Are you all right?" Simon asked, concerned.

"There must be a slight nip in the air. That'll teach me to dress more appropriately for the British weather."

Simon narrowed his eyes, as though he didn't believe her, and opened the car door for her to get in. "Ring me during the day, if you get the chance."

"I will. Have fun with Dad. Don't spend too much money." She bit down on her lip, regretting telling him what he could and couldn't do with his own money. She needn't have worried, though. Simon didn't even react to the words. "See you later."

"Fancy chicken or steak tonight?"

"Steak would be nice. I'll have something light for lunch, if I get the chance to eat, that is."

Sally drove off and looked back in her mirror to see him standing on the steps to his grand manor house that she now considered to be her home as well. It had taken a while.

She put the radio on to accompany her on the journey and arrived at the station within fifteen minutes to find her partner, Jack Blackman, reversing his car into the slot adjacent to hers.

He waved and left his vehicle. Munching on a McMuffin, he asked, "How's it going, Sally?"

"You've got to be kidding? Why are you eating that muck first thing in the morning? Oh, and yes, it's going well, Jack. How about you?"

"Don't start. I need a boost this morning. Another sleepless night due to a teething grandchild, nothing new there. And for your information, there's no need for me to watch my weight. I'm the same weight now as the day the army recruited me at the age of eighteen."

She sniggered at his defensive retort and then gave him a sympathetic smile. "Ouch, poor you. Have you thought about wearing earbuds?"

"Nah, they'd be uncomfortable, can't stand things like that in my ears. I'll survive."

"On the subject of what you choose to eat first thing, I can't believe a man like you, who's keen on exercise and keeping himself fit, would resort to eating shit like that."

They entered Wymondham station and walked up a flight of stairs to the incident room. Jack grumbled all the way behind her. Near the top, he asked, "Hey, when's your honeymoon supposed to start?"

"Simon has to get time off work. He's taking a few days off now, but I mean, it's more difficult to arrange a fortnight off. I have to arrange the same. The whole wedding was an out-of-the-blue thing, as you know."

"Hopefully, you'll be able to get away soon. It would do you good having a break. You seem happy enough."

She laughed. "I am. He's such a sweet man. Don't tell him I told you that, though."

"No fear of that. For your information, men detest being called sweet…just saying."

Sally ran a small team which had been specifically tasked with investigating cold cases with dubious convictions. Predominantly ones that had initially been investigated by a DI Falkirk who had since retired and lost his lucrative pension for dereliction of duty.

Some cases had been harder to deal with than others. So far, they'd successfully released a few innocent prisoners and banged up people who'd thought they'd got away with their crimes for decades. In some respects, their job was a lot harder than if they'd remained in the murder squad. The clues were certainly more difficult to find in a few of the cases. In others, the missed clues had stuck out like sore thumbs.

"Morning, all. Everyone bright and breezy this morning, are we?" she shouted as she entered the incident room.

"I am," Detective Constable Joanna Tryst replied swiftly. No change there then. Joanna was always cheerful around the office.

"So-so for me, boss," Detective Constable Jordan Reid replied, not looking up from his computer screen.

"And what about you, Stuart?" she asked the final member of her team, Detective Constable Stuart McBain, who was thirty-seven but acted a lot older. He was Scottish with a broad accent that Sally sometimes had trouble understanding.

"Aye, fine and dandy, boss. Never better."

"Good. Let me see what awaits me with regard to the post first, and then we'll decide what cases to tackle next."

Jack had already collected a coffee for each of them from the vending machine and handed her a cup which she took into the office. Thankfully, her new role came with less mundane paperwork to sort through, something other inspectors were forced to endure. By the time she'd finished her first coffee of the day, she'd also opened all her mail and dealt with the ten emails awaiting her attention.

She rejoined the rest of the team, and together they went through the files stacked on one side of the office, gathering dust. It had been a few months now since the Cold Case Division had been formed. She was relieved to be working with the same team she'd dealt with before. Although Jack had dug his heels in at the beginning, she felt he was enjoying his role now that they'd managed to arrest a few perps and released a couple of innocent people, such as Craig Gillan, a man who had falsely been accused of killing his own wife. She was still in touch with Craig who was now back with his adult children. They'd bought a property with around ten acres of land, which they'd filled with all sorts of animals, not far from where she lived now. The last she'd heard, Craig had taken delivery of ten more alpacas and was intending to start a breeding programme with them. Sally couldn't be happier at the way his life had turned out. That was why she loved her job so much. Without her team's intervention, the man would have still been wasting away in prison. He'd given up any hope of getting out alive before she and her team had plucked his case from the pile.

"You've gone quiet. I know what that means. You're thinking about Gillan again, aren't you?" Jack yelled across the room. His chair was tilted back, balancing on two legs.

"Spot on. That case always gladdens my heart and is an excellent reminder why we must continue to plough through the rest of them. So, here goes. Joanna, is there anything that has caught your eye recently?"

"I made a note about something last week that rang a bell. I set it to one side to complete the paperwork on the Ryland case. Hang on... Ah, here it is."

Sally approached her and perched on the spare desk next to the constables.

"I remembered seeing a story featured on the local news last week about this case. The reporter interviewed the mother of a child who was murdered nineteen years ago. The news team wanted to highlight the case as it was coming up to the twentieth anniversary. I came in the following day to see if the case was one of those in our care, and it was. I meant to say something to you about it, but to be honest, it slipped my mind."

"Don't go beating yourself up. We've all had a lot on our plate with the Ryland case. That was a complex one for us to deal with. This sounds a heartbreaker of an investigation. Do you want to tell us what you know?"

Joanna smiled, swallowed and left her seat. She approached the whiteboard and spoke as she jotted some names down on the board. Sally sat in Joanna's chair and crossed her arms. The rest of the team listened in silence as Joanna revealed the true extent of the crime.

"So, we have the mother, Anna Pickrel, who was thirty-three at the time of her daughter's death. What I gleaned from the interview is that she is riddled with guilt."

"Why?" Sally asked, leaning forward in her chair and resting her elbows on the desk.

"Apparently, Anna was out on a date that night with a new fella. She left her two children, Millie, aged six, and Louie, aged twelve, in the care of a sixteen-year-old babysitter, a girl called Lisa. During the evening, Lisa received an emergency call from her mother telling her that her father had suffered a heart attack. Lisa contacted Anna immediately. Anna urged Lisa to leave the children and also said that she would be home right away."

"Okay, so how did the child end up being murdered?" Sally asked, her brow twisting into a deep frown. It was hard for her to fathom any mother telling a babysitter to leave her children alone in the house.

"When Anna arrived, there was an ambulance at the house, paramedics performing CPR on the girl, but they were too late. Louie was in bits. He had the foresight to ring nine-nine-nine when he found a man standing over his sister, smothering her with a pillow. He shouted. The man clearly thought the girl was alone in the house, and he bolted."

"Hang on, back up a second. So are we to gather that this bloke just walked in off the street and targeted this little girl? A stalker? Had he been watching the house? Wait, what about the phone call from the babysitter, was it genuine?"

"Yes, Lisa's father died that night along with Millie."

"Shit! That's terrible. Horrendous situation for all concerned. There are a lot of unanswered questions to this case from what I can tell. Where was Louie at the time of the attack?"

"He shared a room with his sister. He'd gone to the toilet and came back to find the man attacking his sister. Well, attacking might be a poor choice of words—*killing* his sister, I should say."

"Jesus, the poor lad. He must have been traumatised by the events. I can't believe he held it together enough to ring the emergency services. He has to be admired. Was he interviewed by the journalist at the same time as his mother last week?"

"No. His mother told the journalist that they were both full of guilt and remorse about the incident. They were a loving family. Apparently, the day Millie was murdered, they'd spent the day at the pool together in Great Yarmouth, her way of making it up to the kids for leaving them to go on the date."

"I've heard enough. I think we should take this case on. Who's with me on that one?"

The team all nodded, except for Jack.

Here we go again! "Jack? What say you?"

He stretched out his arms and placed his hands behind his head. "Well, for what it's worth, yes, I agree it's going to be a tough case for us to entertain, even tougher if there is no DNA evidence to go on. Is there, Joanna?"

She returned to the nearby desk where she'd left the file and shook her head. "No, nothing. Which probably baffled DI Falkirk and his team at the time."

Sally raised a hand. "Stop! We're so much better than them. That shouldn't deter us in the slightest. We've already proven how efficient we are with these cold cases. I say we tackle this one, give that girl and her family the justice they're seeking and deserve. Bloody hell, nearly twenty years. You know what I find galling? The fact that I've never even heard of the case. Can any of you recall it?"

Joanna shook her head. "Not until last week. I'm with you, boss. Most of these cases we've heard about in the distant past, but this one, well, nothing came to mind at all, not until I looked into it. Heartbreaking, isn't it? It would be great if we could solve this one for the family."

"I agree. Want to give me a show of hands, team?"

Everyone raised their hands in support. She looked Jack's way, and he was staring at the floor. "Jack?"

He shrugged his broad shoulders. "If it's a path you want to take, then who am I to argue with you?"

Same old Jack, digging his heels in at first. She chose to ignore him. "Okay, folks, you know the drill. We need to read through the entire investigation, see who was questioned and when. Then we'll have to track those people down and interview them a second time. I know we're talking almost twenty years here, but would people truly forget what happened back then in the circumstances? I'm guessing not. Joanna, can you find me an address for the mother? That should be our first stop, to go and see her. Not that I'm looking forward to it. I think this case is going to be an emotional roller-coaster of a ride for all of us."

"I'll search for her address now, boss. Do you want the son's address, too?"

"Good idea, and any other relatives living in the area as well, but that can be researched over the next day or two. Let's stick with the immediate family for now."

"Will do, boss," Joanna replied, heading back to her seat.

"Stuart and Jordan, I'd like you to try and trace the babysitter and any possible neighbours at the time. Glancing through the file, which should be a darn sight thicker, I'm guessing the neighbours and anyone else living on the street at the time weren't interviewed very well. Why am I not surprised by that? Also, we need to research any possible connections to other crimes of this nature in that area around the same time. Again, a quick glimpse through the file, and I'm not seeing anything along those lines at all. Jesus, what was Falkirk thinking? By the look of things, this investigation took up a few weeks max of his team's time. If anybody else was involved I'd make excuses for them, the possibility of yet another major crime coming in that took them away from the case, but we're talking about an inspector who was not on top of his game."

"Makes you wonder what was going on back then, doesn't it?" Jack said.

"With regard to him being accountable to his superiors, you mean, like I am? It beggars belief. I know that's not the bloody first, or last time, I'm going to say that either when we tackle these cases. What were they all thinking back then? Doesn't a family, a desperate mother, deserve to have her child's murder investigated fully? Crap, sorry, my anger is showing again. Seriously, can you imagine any of us getting away with neglecting our duty?"

"No, I'd see to that," the voice of DCI Mike Green boomed behind her.

Sally swiftly turned to face him. "Sorry, sir, you weren't supposed to hear that."

"It's okay, I understand your frustrations, Inspector. A word in your office, if I may?"

Sally turned back to address her team. "Okay, you each have a task to be getting on with. Jack, do a rough background check on the mother and son for me in readiness for our visit later."

Jack nodded, and Sally walked into her office, closely followed by DCI Green who constantly popped in to check how things were progressing with her and her team. It was a shame the DCI at the time wasn't as hands-on during Falkirk's reign as inspector. Maybe there wouldn't have been a need to set up the cold case team. Sally sank into her chair and motioned for her boss to sit opposite her. "What can I do for you, sir?"

"Nothing really. Just doing my usual, making my presence felt and to assure you that I'm here if you need me. I take it you're about to begin another case. Care to enlighten me as to what it is?"

Sally ran through the details of the Pickrel case.

All the while, Green shook his head in disgust. "Sickening that this family has been neglected by this station over the years. Make sure you pull out all the stops on this one, Parker. Oops…that is still your name, or is it?"

"For the moment, sir. I thought it would be better not to confuse things at work."

"Given your background with your ex-husband, I would have thought you'd have pounced on the chance to change it, although I can understand the hassle doing that would give you. I'll keep my nose out of your personal affairs."

"In truth, I can't wait to get rid of Darryl's name, sir. I thought I'd do all the personal stuff first and then take on Bracknall at work in the next few months, unless you think I should do it all at the same time."

Green held his hands up in front of him. "Count me out of the decision-making process. Won't it be odd using your married name along with your partner's?"

Sally frowned. "In what way, sir?"

"When you're out and about on a case and you introduce yourselves, Bracknall and Blackman?"

Sally laughed. "The thought hadn't crossed my mind, sir. It does sound like a firm of solicitors, doesn't it?"

He offered a weak smile which was all she ever received from him. "Indeed. The choice is yours. Let me know when you decide to make the change. Back to this case… How likely are you to solve it after all this time?"

"We won't know that for a few days, if not more, sir. It's still in its infancy. Jack and I will visit the family today. I have to say I fear this one is going to be one of our toughest cases yet."

"After hearing the facts, I'm inclined to agree with you. I'll be off, let you get on. Keep me up to date on this one. I know I say that with every case you investigate, but I'm interested in where this one in particular leads."

"Any reason why, sir?"

He rose from his seat. "You get a gut reaction about some cases more than others. I think that's what's happening here. Don't worry, I won't pester you any more than usual. I know you'll do your best, you always do."

Sally followed him out of the office, her cheeks warming because of the unexpected subtle praise he'd bestowed upon her. "Thank you, sir."

"Carry on, team," he shouted over his shoulder as he left the room.

Sally let out a relieved sigh. She hated it when Green showed up unannounced. "Okay, where were we?"

"We've got the address for Anna Forbes—yes, she's now remarried. Her son has still remained Louie Pickrel, though." Jack said.

"A recent marriage perhaps? We'll soon find out. Let's go."

2

Jack insisted on driving to the location. Anna Forbes lived in a row of newly built detached houses on the edge of Acle, with the river running along the back of the property.

Joanna had paved the way for their visit, ringing ahead to notify Mrs Forbes they would be there shortly. She was looking out of the bay window, waiting for them to show up, when Jack drew up outside the house.

He ducked down to view the house from the driver's seat. "Nice pad."

"I love it around here. I hope the developers don't spoil it by building dozens of new homes."

"They will. They always do. There's a housing shortage, remember."

"I know. It concerns me when they throw up homes willy-nilly and don't consider the impact it has on a community."

"Get you. Are we going in, or do you want to sit here discussing something that is totally out of our hands?"

"Don't you care what happens in our community, Jack?"

"Not really. I live a good twenty miles from here so I don't class this as my community."

Sally sighed. "And that's where the problem lies."

"Meaning what?"

"People don't care enough. The planners probably feel the same way as you do."

"Can I remind you we have a case to investigate?"

"Sorry, okay. I'm back with the programme now."

They exited the car to find Anna Forbes holding the front door open for them. Sally introduced herself and Jack and then entered the property. Anna led the way to a large kitchen-diner at the rear of the house. The view out into the garden revealed that although the sides had fences erected, there was nothing to block the view of the river at the bottom.

"This is lovely. Is that a jetty I can see?" Sally asked.

Anna came to admire the view beside her. "Yes, my husband is a keen sailor. Our boat is in for its annual service at the moment. We usually have it moored up here. Would you like a tea or coffee?"

"Coffee for me, thank you. Jack?"

"And one for me, too, thanks."

Anna smiled and switched on the kettle she'd already boiled in anticipation of their visit. Within seconds the drinks were made. "Please, take a seat at the table."

Sally and Jack sat on a bench on one side of the table. Anna carried a tray and distributed the mugs then placed a bowl of sugar and a plate of chocolate digestives between them. She made herself comfortable on the other side of the table and wrapped her hands around her mug.

"Okay, first of all, Mrs Forbes…"

Mrs Forbes interrupted her. "Please, call me Anna."

"Thank you. As I was saying, before we get down to the nitty-gritty, I'd like to give you a little background information as to why we're here. My team has recently been formed to investigate several cases that have been highlighted over the years. One of those cases is yours."

"What you're telling me in a roundabout way is that the investigating officer screwed up and you've been tasked with clearing up his mess."

"That's about it in a nutshell. However, I also want to assure you that during our time working on the cold case team, we've had major success in the cases we've reinvestigated. I don't mean to raise your hopes by telling you that. All I'm trying to do is reassure you that you'll be in safe hands this time around and to apologise for the way the police have failed you in the past. It's unforgiveable. We'll do everything we can to make up for your past disappointment and hopefully achieve our aim, to give you the outcome you and your family deserve."

"Thank you, that means a lot. We were treated abysmally by the inspector in charge in those days. He never took our claims seriously back then. I got the impression that he was punishing me for leaving the children alone. I would never have done that ordinarily. There was an emergency, something neither Dean or I could have accounted for. My children always came first." Her gaze drifted over to the shelf beside Sally.

Sally followed Anna's gaze to a photo of two happy children. The photo was a little dark and dated.

"Is that Millie?" she asked.

"Yes, that's my darling daughter. I know every mother will tell you their children were or are angels, but she truly was. I never had to tell her off, ever. Both children were good from day one in my eyes."

"That's lovely to hear. I must admit, it does make a change. If it's not too much trouble, maybe you could go over the events of that evening as you remember them."

"They're seared into my memory. I will never forget them as long as I'm walking this earth. The guilt still pricks my soul every day." She bowed her head, gazing at her mug, and retold what had gone on that evening. Once she'd finished, she glanced up at Sally, her eyes brimming with tears, and said, "I remember it as if it were yesterday. There are some things in this life you can never forget, no matter how hard you try. And believe me, over the past nineteen years, I've tried my hardest to let it go and failed."

"I'm so sorry this is still affecting you so deeply. They say time is a great healer. I guess in certain cases that simply isn't true. Believe me when I tell you that we'll do our very best to get to the bottom of what went on that night. Do you think your son will be up to speaking to us? As he was there at the time, it would be better if we went through the events in more detail with him."

"He's aware that you will want to speak with him and has told me he'd be willing to go over the traumatic details once more if it means bringing this case to a satisfactory conclusion. In truth, I can't believe this is happening after all these years of neglect by the police. The fact is that there is a murderer out there, walking the streets of Norfolk, and yet very little has been done to apprehend that person in the past two decades. No, let me correct that statement, *nothing*, absolutely zero has been done to find the culprit. Tell me, before you picked up the file, were you even aware of my daughter's murder?"

Sally shook her head and gulped. "I asked my team the same question before we came here this morning, and none of them had any prior knowledge of the case, which is shocking in itself. Again, I can only apologise for the way you and your family have been treated in the past. It shouldn't have happened, and yes, you're right, the fact that a murderer has been allowed to walk the streets since the incident occurred is…well, grossly unacceptable and totally abhorrent. I can't make up for the way you and your son were treated back then but, going forward, my team and I will do everything we can to ensure we bring justice to your door and put an end to the torment you have had to endure over the years."

"Thank you. I hope you're right. Nineteen years, though? The murderer might not be around these parts now. Worse still, he or she might even be dead for all we know. Anything could have happened to them since then."

"Exactly. I'm not going to say this investigation is going to be easy; however, we possibly have more resources this time around. If that sounds like an excuse for what went on in the past, it wasn't meant to be. What I'm saying is, now that a dedicated team has been set up to deal with these cases, there's every chance we'll be able to solve it this time. Although, as you rightly say, the guilty party might be lying six feet under by now, and all this might be a waste of time. Except it won't be, because then you'll have a resolution, closure, if you like."

"If an unsatisfactory one, that's what you're saying, yes?"

Sally nodded. "Yes. The unfortunate thing is the lack of DNA evidence found at the scene. I should imagine that would have caused an initial stumbling block for the original investigation."

"I know. The kill…the person responsible must have seriously thought about the crime before he committed it. He must've been watching the house. That's always been my suspicion, one that useless copper didn't want to hear about back then."

"I'm inclined to agree with you. Can you cast your mind back—perhaps you can recall falling out with someone around that time, possibly on the lookout for some form of retribution?"

"Not that I can recall. I'd just started a new job and I was out on my first date. The children's father was banged up in prison. You know what, I had my suspicions he was behind it at one point, but Falkirk virtually laughed in my face when I suggested it."

Jack took out his notebook and scribbled something in it.

"We'll look into it. Do you know if he's still in prison now?"

"No, I lost track of him. Sebastian Randall is his name. If he is out now, walking the streets, then I have to say I haven't laid eyes on him and he's never once contacted his son."

"Leave that with us. We'll chase it up when we get back to the station. I feel it's something that should have been checked on at the time. Prisoners have contacts on the outside, so someone could have easily been persuaded to act on your ex-partner's behalf." As Sally knew full well herself. Darryl had done the very same thing to her not so long ago. She shuddered as the memories filled her mind.

She saw Jack look her way out of the corner of her eye and turned to give him a reassuring smile, letting him know she was fine.

Sally noticed a few more photos scattered around the room. "You're married now. Do you have any other children?"

"That's right, and yes." She pointed to the photo of a young boy with a toothy smile. "My son, our son, is called Callum. He's a darling boy. I'm very protective of him. I check him constantly through the night. I don't tend to sleep much nowadays. Every time I close my eyes I see Millie's face, a tortured expression, and she's reaching out to me with her tiny arms. She's so far in the distance, and as I move towards her, something swoops down and carries her farther away from me. I'll never touch her again, not even in my dreams or nightmares. I've had hundreds of them over the years, reliving the horrendous events of that evening. I'm standing at the bottom of the bed, watching the man suffocating my beautiful child, and there's little I can do to prevent it. I'm glued to the spot. The faceless man laughs, it's more of a witch's cackle, actually, and continues to suck the life out of my daughter. I can't shake the images from my head. It's why I rarely sleep. I've taken part in so many experiments to try and cure me, even enrolled at the local university a few years back to see if they could help me. No such luck. I'm permanently exhausted. I can't hold down a job as my mental capacity is virtually non-existent. I look and feel like a zombie most days. It's only the love of a good man and my son—sorry, sons—that keeps me going."

Sally took a closer look at the woman. Dark circles around her eyes were the most prominent feature on her pretty yet ageing face. "I'm sorry. I know this sounds an inadequate thing to say in the circumstances, but I regret wholeheartedly the way you've been treated by the police over the years and promise to make amends for the heartbreak you have suffered."

"I don't blame you. I can't even blame the investigating officer at the time, not really. All the pain and torment I have been subjected to is the fault of the person who stole my daughter away from me. Losing her stripped me of so much. I thought having Callum would ease some of that pain. It hasn't. That doesn't mean that I love him any less than I should." She held a clenched fist over her heart. "There's a gaping wound in my chest which will never heal, not while I'm still alive.

Sometimes I lay there in bed at night and pray that God takes me. I can't explain the magnitude of that pain. No one will ever understand. Only another mother who has lost her child will recognise the anguishing pain running through me. Nearly twenty years later, and the pain has grown worse over the years."

Sally listened as tears pricked her eyes. Anna was right. No one could imagine the pain brought to a parent who has lost a child. Jack cleared his throat beside her, apparently struggling to keep his own emotions in check. As much as Sally detested veering the subject indirectly away from the woman's own torment, she was eager to learn more about that evening. "Going back to that night, am I to understand you were on a date?"

Anna's gaze dropped to her mug once more. She turned it in her hands a few times and then answered. "I was. It's my biggest regret."

"Why? You were entitled to have a life of your own."

"It was the first time I'd ever left the children. That in itself carries a dreadful burden."

"I didn't know that. I can imagine. No one could have foreseen what would happen that evening. Maybe the intruder would have still broken into your house even if you were at home. Have you considered that over the years?"

"I've thought about it, but it hasn't prevented me from punishing myself. Have you ever felt guilt about something in your life, Inspector?"

Sally paused to reflect. She couldn't place anything that had occurred in her life, except the time her dog, Dex, had gone missing for a few minutes. As it turned out, one of Darryl's cronies from prison had dognapped him, tied him up and placed duct tape around his snout. Luckily, she'd found him before any lasting damage had been done to him. The guilt had remained with her for a few weeks. She hadn't let him out of her sight on walks after that. "Nothing in comparison to what you've experienced, Anna. I've only had a brief chance to sift through the case files. Can you tell me what the police did for you, on that night and in the following days?"

"Not a lot really, or should I say, if they did, I was in too much of a daze to comprehend it. Louie was a tower of strength. Despite his own grief, he persuaded the officer in charge to liaise with him."

"Really? That's very strange. Your son was underage at the time, if I recall?"

"He was twelve. We were very close, still are. He's always been a considerate child. He did his best to ease the situation for me. It wasn't until years had passed that I sat back and considered that was the wrong thing to have done. Maybe if I had pestered the police daily, perhaps then they might have pulled out all the stops to find the murderer. That's yet another regret to add to the others I've experienced over the years. I sit here most days going over the events and try to come up with a solution, but…well, I've resigned myself now to living a tormented life until the day I die."

"Is that fair on your new husband and your younger son? I don't mean that disrespectfully."

Her gaze met Sally's. "It is what it is. I'm unable to switch off my feelings. I have a very patient husband who loves the bones of me. He's tormented by grief himself as he feels partially responsible."

"May I ask why?" Sally wondered, thinking it an odd thing for Anna to say.

"Because he should have met me sooner. He believes if he had, Millie would still be with us today. Maybe he's right, I don't know."

"No one can tell you if that's true or not. The man entered the house that evening; do you know how he got in?"

"I don't. Louie reckoned it was through an open window at the rear of the property. I ensured the window in my bedroom was closed that night before I went out. I should have checked the children's room. I didn't. Something else for me to feel guilty about. I was too caught up in my own excitement. I had first-date nerves and yet I still had to make sure the babysitter and the children had everything they needed in my absence. I remembered running around like the proverbial headless chicken that evening. My date arrived at seven. We left virtually straight away, although I did introduce him to the kids."

"How did that go?"

"Really well. The kids appeared to take to him instantly. It boded well for the future, providing the date went according to plan, that is."

"And did it?"

"Yes, Dean and I had a wonderful meal, until…the phone call came through from Lisa. The poor girl was beside herself that evening. As soon as she told me what had happened to her father, I didn't have any hesitation in telling her to leave. She locked the door after her. Dean rushed me back to the house; we broke a few speed limits on the way." Her cheeks flushed with colour at the admission. "When we arrived, I was gobsmacked to see the ambulance sitting outside the house. I ran inside to find the paramedic compressing Millie's chest, trying to get her heart to spark back into life. It was too late."

"Did Dean follow you into the house?"

"Yes. I was traumatised; I told him to go. I shouted at him, I believe. I haven't seen him since that night."

"That's a shame. How did you meet him?"

"At work. I'd not long started a new job. We got on well."

"That must have been awkward when you returned to work?"

"I never went back. I sent them my resignation by post that week. I couldn't have coped at work and I haven't worked since that day. I wouldn't be able to concentrate. Every thought of every day consists of Millie. I know an outsider would find that hard to believe, but it's the truth."

"I completely understand. May I ask how you met your current husband?"

"At school, a parents' evening. He'd recently lost his wife. He has a daughter; she's eighteen now and at university. He was riddled with grief at the time. I suppose that drew us together. That's why he understands how I feel and the guilt I carry with me daily."

"That's such a shame. I'm so pleased you found each other, though, and that you went on to have another child."

A smile touched her lips. "He's a blessing in disguise. I try my hardest to remain positive when Callum is around, so does Malcolm. Once our son is in bed, we both become maudlin again. Sounds stupid that we're capable of switching our emotions off when other people are around, as if to shield them. Oh, I don't know, again, it's impossible to explain."

"I take it you've had some form of counselling over the years?"

"Yes and no. I tried a few times. The counsellors asked stupid questions, and I clammed up. I didn't have an affinity with them, found it hard to open up, so I refused to go again. Maybe that was the wrong thing to do, I don't know."

"It's not too late, it's never too late to try. It might be worth giving it another shot. Find a counsellor with whom you feel comfortable. I could ask around for you, if that's what you want?"

"Let me think about it, and I'll get back to you."

"I wouldn't want to push you into doing something you wouldn't feel comfortable with. However, it's been almost twenty years you've been punishing yourself. You have to ask the question whether Millie would want you to waste your life like that." Sally cringed. Had she gone too far? Pushed Anna too much too soon?

Anna's expression altered between one of severe pain to one of thoughtfulness. In the end, she nodded slightly. "Maybe you have a point. Perhaps it would be better to try one last time than to continue to live in this nightmare state. I'll give it some serious thought and talk it over with my husband this evening."

"If you're both suffering with guilt, perhaps you should suggest that you both go and see the counsellor."

"We'll see. Is there anything else you need to speak to me about regarding that night?"

"I just have a few more questions, and then we'll leave you in peace. How long had you known the babysitter, Lisa?"

She let out a long sigh and shook her head. "Before that evening, not much. Her mother worked at the same office and offered Lisa's services to me once she found out I had accepted the invitation for the date. She was a lovely girl, though. She came around to spend a few hours with the kids the prior weekend, to make sure she wasn't a complete stranger on the night. Louie said she was lovely with them during the hour or so she was there. If she'd been horrible, he would have told me. We didn't have any secrets."

"I see. She must've been torn up once she learnt what had happened to Millie."

"She was. Despite losing her own father that night, the following day she turned up on the doorstep and broke down. I'm still in contact with her today, and she still carries the burden of guilt around with her. I've told her she shouldn't, but she's such a sensitive soul. She even came to the funeral. It wasn't much. A few local residents turned up to pay their respects, you know, close neighbours, a couple of teachers from Millie's school. I appreciated them all attending—that was until that blasted reporter showed up. Louie was furious with him, shoved him away once he started taking photos of Millie's tiny coffin lying in the grave. It spoilt the day. I wanted to give my princess the send-off she deserved, and it turned into a farce. The journalist later apologised, but by then, the damage had been done."

"Do you remember the journalist's name? I know it's asking a lot from you."

"A Todd Stockman, or Stockard perhaps. I think that was his name. Either one of those anyway."

"We'll try and find the information when we get back to the station."

"Can I ask why you'd want to know that?"

Sally shrugged. "The more people we speak to, the better chance we have of getting to the truth, even after all these years. It's what we do and how we've achieved convictions to the other cold crime cases we've dealt with in the past few months."

"I see. I don't have a clue if he's still a journalist or if he's still in the area."

"You don't have to worry about that. Have you remained in contact with your old neighbours?"

"I can't say I have. I wanted to cut all the ties I had from back then. I only stayed in contact with Lisa because I felt guilty about her father dying that night within hours of Millie going."

"I understand. Maybe you can go through what Inspector Falkirk told you about the investigation, if you're up to it?"

She shook her head. "Not really. He barely spoke to me after that fateful night. Whenever I chased the progress on the case, he always ensured that my call never got past his partner. He quoted he was a very busy man on the trail of a child killer, as if I wasn't aware of that fact. I found him to be rude and arrogant. I'm not surprised he cocked up cases and that you've had to reopen them. He was a waste of space from what I could tell. Louie hated him, couldn't stand the bloke from the minute he laid eyes on him."

"That's awful. I hope you can tell, I'll give your daughter's case my best shot."

"I can sense you're a kind-hearted and compassionate person and caring police officer."

"Thank you. I think it's always better to have a good rapport with a family member in incidents such as this. Without your help, solving the crime will be a darn sight harder."

"I agree to help when and where I can. The problem is that I don't know much more than what I've told you already. I don't recall anyone lingering around the house the previous week. I sometimes wish I had because then I would have a picture of the killer in my head."

"If you'd seen him, we could have done a line-up or created a photofit of the perpetrator."

"Louie did that at the time."

Sally and Jack glanced at each other and frowned.

"You seem surprised by that news. Wasn't it in the file?"

"Not that I can recall, although, to be fair, I only took a brief look through it before we set off to come and see you this morning. I'll make a note to search it properly upon our return. Was the E-FIT ever circulated through the media?"

"I suppose it must have been. I honestly can't remember. Louie did his best, and it never seemed good enough for Falkirk."

Sally heaved out a sigh and shook her head. "Does your son still live in the area?"

"Yes, he's currently away on business for a few days. He's a salesman for a paint company. He's due to ring me tonight. I can tell him to contact you, to arrange a meeting, if that's what you want?"

"That would be excellent. The sooner, the better. It's important we get all the facts from him as soon as possible. Can I ask how his state of mind is after all these years?"

She hitched up a shoulder. "He's a man, they cope better than women. Saying that, Malcolm hasn't coped too well about his wife in the past. He's getting better, though."

"I'm glad to hear that. What sort of relationship does your son have with his half-brother?"

"The best kind possible. He'll never be as close as he was to Millie; however, he adores Callum. Insists Callum stays with him some weekends to give me and Malcolm some time alone together. At times, I don't know what I would have done without Louie being around to comfort me. He's grown up to be a fine young man in spite of what this cruel life has thrown at him."

"Is he in a relationship?"

"Yes, he's married, and they're expecting their first child. I couldn't be more thrilled for them both. Natalie is a wonderful girl. They've been married for two years. He worships her, can't do enough for her. She was a model until she fell pregnant. They've told me that if they have a girl, they're going to call her Millie."

Sally cringed—not something she would relish; it would act as a permanent reminder, not that Anna was likely to forget her dead child. "How do you feel about that, Anna?"

"In some respects, I think it would be a beautiful tribute to his sister, whom he cherished, but other times, I struggle to get my mind around it. To me, there will only ever be one Millie Pickrel."

"Maybe if it's going to upset you, it might be worth having a word with your son or possibly his wife. I'm sure she'll understand."

"I'll cope with it, if I have to. I'm really not one for rocking the boat. It's a loving gesture on Louie's part."

"Okay, if that's how you feel. Is there anything else you think we should look into that wasn't covered in the initial investigation?"

She turned her head to the side, glanced at her daughter's photo and chewed on her lip. "I don't think so."

Sally withdrew a card from her jacket pocket and slid it across the table. "I'm going to leave you a card. If you think of anything once we're gone, don't hesitate to ring me. Also, if you wouldn't mind asking Louie to give me a call to arrange a suitable time for an interview, I'd appreciate it."

"Of course. I'll show you out."

The three of them rose from their chairs and made their way back to the front door. Sally held out her hand for Anna to shake.

Once they were back in the car, Jack pulled away from the house and parked up again in the next street. "Where do we go from here?" he asked, turning in his seat to face her.

"I'm going to ring the station, see if Joanna can give me the lowdown on the ex before I do anything else."

Jack fiddled with his own mobile while Sally placed the call on hers.

"Joanna, it's me. I need you to get me some background information on Anna Forbes' ex-partner, Sebastian Randall. As far as Anna is concerned, he was in prison at the time of her daughter's death. I'd like to know where he is now."

"I'll get on it right away and ring you back, boss."

"Thanks." Sally hung up. "Let's find a café somewhere. No point in starting off in another direction just yet."

By the time Jack had sourced a nearby coffee shop, Joanna had the information for Sally. "Hit me with it," Sally said.

"Sebastian Randall would appear to be a serial offender. Over the past twenty years, he's been released no fewer than six times and ended back inside within a day or two."

"Interesting. Okay, where's he at now?"

"Norwich prison. Recently went to court on a burglary charge and got two years for his trouble."

"Thanks. Maybe he's the type who struggles to exist on the outside world."

"Seems that way."

"Thanks, Joanna. Can you search through his file for me, see where he was at the time of Millie's death?"

The ruffling sound of paper filled the line. "Ah, yes, he was inside doing an eighteen-month stretch for ABH."

"Interesting, so he's been banged up on different charges then."

"So it would appear. Want me to continue digging for you?"

"If you would. Be in touch soon." She ended the call and took a sip of her coffee as she thought. "We'll have this, then I'll see if I can contact the governor of Norwich prison, if I can remember his damn name…ah, yes, I think it was Ward. He was new to his position last year."

"Thinking of going to see Randall?" Jack asked, bolting down the remains of his sugary doughnut.

"Yep. If there's a chance he was behind his daughter's death, then we'll get it out of him."

"Ya think? I'm not so sure. What would his motive be?"

Sally shrugged. "Who knows with these guys? I'm not saying he was behind it but I can't just leave it, Jack."

"I understand. Sounds like you're already getting frustrated with this one." He picked up another doughnut and took a huge chunk out of it.

"You're not wrong there. Bloody hell, that's your second one. Where do you put it all? It's only a few hours since you had your McMuffin, for fuck's sake."

"I'll work it off when I get home."

Sally raised her hand to stop him saying anything more. "Too much information."

"Ha! As if. The days of me going home to ravage Donna after a long shift are a thing of the past, what with two older children and a grandchild at home. Anyway, you've got a one-track mind. I meant I would burn it off down at the gym."

Sally pulled a face. "Oops, sorry."

"Just because you're still in the honeymoon period in your relationship, it doesn't mean to say everyone else is."

"All right, you don't have to bleat on about it." She picked up her phone and dialled a number she had stored in it. "Hi, sorry to trouble you. This is DI Sally Parker calling from the Norfolk Constabulary."

"Hello there. What can I do for you?" the governor's cheery secretary asked.

"I know it's short notice, but I was wondering if Governor Ward could fit me in for a brief visit today."

"Let me check his diary. Hmm…he appears to have a spare half an hour just after lunch at two-fifteen. Is that any good for you?"

"Marvellous. Can you put me down for that?"

"Already done. See you then, Inspector."

3

Governor Ward welcomed Sally and Jack into his office. "Nice to see you again, Inspector."

"You, too, sir. It's been a few months," Sally added with a laugh.

"I'm glad to see you with a smile on your face after your distasteful past experiences with your ex. Oh, wait, I had some news about him the other day, where is it?" He hunted through the files on his desk until he found the correct one.

Sally's stomach tied itself into knots. *What the hell has Darryl been up to now?*

Governor Ward flipped the cover open and used his finger to search for what he was looking for on the page. "Here it is. I'm not sure what your reaction is going to be when you hear this."

She closed her eyes, bracing herself for the worst news possible, that the prison had decided to release him early on good behaviour. Jack placed a hand on her arm, and she flinched.

"Are you all right? You look like you're gonna faint," he asked, concerned.

She gave him a reassuring smile. "I'll let you know after I've heard the news. Go on, Governor Ward."

"Apparently, Darryl got into a fight with another inmate and ended up in hospital."

She gasped. "Oh God, don't tell me he's escaped from the hospital he was transferred to."

Governor Ward smiled. "No, nothing like that."

She let out the breath she'd sucked in. "What then?"

"He did have a spell in hospital while they fixed his busted hip."

"Ouch!" Jack said. "Couldn't have happened to a nicer guy."

Sally smiled and let out a relieved sigh. "He's safely tucked up in his cell again now, though, right?"

"He is," the governor confirmed.

"Good. Now that's out of the way, the reason for our visit today is to enquire if you'll allow us to see one of your prisoners. It's relating to a cold case we're investigating."

"I don't see why not. You know I'm always happy to oblige. Which prisoner are we talking about here?"

"Sebastian Randall."

The governor frowned as he tried to recall the name. "Nope, it's not ringing any bells. Let me try and locate his file for you." He left his desk and crossed the room to the metal filing cabinets lining one wall. He opened the second drawer down on the first one he came to. "Randall, ah, yes." He took the file out and shut the drawer again. After retaking his seat, he flipped the file open. "He likes doing the hokey cokey. In, out, in, out. We've got a few prisoners like him."

"Any known reason why they prefer being inside?" Sally asked. She had her own idea, but it would be good to hear the views of an expert.

"Most of these guys don't know anything else in this life. When they get out of here, they seem to freak out. A lot of them have been cast aside by their families. They have no place to call home, no money except the pittance we give them once we turf them out. No chance of finding a job with no fixed abode. Weigh it up for yourself—they either find a cardboard box somewhere and freeze to death or commit another crime that is likely to end in a prison sentence. At least they know they get regular meals and a relatively comfy bed to sleep in during their stay here."

"It's a harsh reality check, isn't it? Makes you feel sorry for them in a way."

"I agree. It's hard to judge someone when it's laid out to you like that. There just isn't the support out there these days for people who reoffend."

"How many prisoners do you have that fit into that category?" Sally asked out of interest.

"Off the top of my head, I'd say that figure is likely to be around fifty."

"That's harsh to think that our society is failing them."

"Not everyone sees it that way; however, I'm inclined to agree with you. It's all about the cutbacks, no matter which way we turn. One thing it doesn't solve is the overcrowding of the prisons."

"There is that."

"Now we've put the world to rights, let me arrange for you to see this man. May I ask what the cold case is?"

"Actually, it's the death of his daughter, Millie."

"I see. I'm not aware of the case. Poor man. Something like that might be the reason he prefers to remain behind bars. Perhaps his emotional state is hard to deal with when he's on the outside."

"It's certainly something that hadn't crossed my mind."

He nodded and placed a call to another department. "They're collecting him and taking him to an interview room now."

"Thanks, much appreciated. We'll be gentle with him, I promise."

"You don't have to promise that. I trust you. Let me show you the way."

Sally smirked. "I think I can remember that by now."

"No doubt."

The three of them left the governor's office and wound their way through the narrow corridors to the interview rooms. Sally and Jack entered the room to find a man with long grey hair tied back in a ponytail, already seated at the table. He was wearing jeans and a white T-shirt. A prison officer was standing erect against the back wall.

Two chairs had been placed opposite the prisoner. Sally and Jack sat at the table.

"Hello, Mr Randall. Is it all right if I call you Sebastian? I'm DI Sally Parker, and this is my partner, DS Jack Blackman."

"I prefer to be called Seb. What's this about?"

Sally peered into his light-blue eyes and saw nothing but sorrow, making her think this visit would be a waste of time. "Nothing to be concerned about. We'd just like to ask you a few questions about a cold case we've reopened."

He tilted his head and frowned. "What cold case? Nothing to do with what I've done over the years. I was convicted for all the crimes I committed. If you've come to hassle me about anything else, then I have to tell you you're barking up the wrong tree."

"No, it doesn't concern any crimes you've committed." *At least I don't think it does now that I've met you, but here goes anyway.* "Actually, I have to inform you that we've reopened the case of your daughter's murder."

His hands clenched and unclenched on the table in front of him, and then he ran both of them through his hair, loosening some of the strands from the ponytail. "Jesus, after all these years, you're finally doing the decent thing. I can't believe what I'm hearing."

"I hope this time round we'll find the perpetrator."

"I'm confused. Why come to see me? You think I know who the likely perp is because of where I lay my head at night?"

"Perhaps, although that's not the real reason behind our visit."

"I don't understand. What else can I tell you? I was banged up in here the night she...died."

"I know, we've read your record. If you bear with me, I'd like to get some more background information about you and your family, if that's all right?"

"I wasn't with them at the time. That bitch ran out on me, said I hit her."

"And did you?"

"I might've lashed out once when she nagged me for being drunk, but all men do that when pushed, don't they?"

"No, they don't," Jack was quick to respond.

"I agree with my partner, not all men hit their wives." Although Darryl had beaten her to a pulp and even gone further on more than one occasion. She was with a decent man now. Simon had never once caused her to think he was anything but a caring, gentle man. Was he one of a kind, though?

"I lost my job, and she kept bending me ear about it. I snapped and hit her. I regretted my actions, but it was too late. She took the kids and left without telling me where they were. I ended up turning to crime because of that bitch."

"Seriously? You blame your ex-partner for your failings as a human being?"

"Hark at you. Don't judge me unless you've been in my shoes, lady."

"Whatever. The day you found out about your daughter's death, can you run me through your emotions?"

He sat forward. "Is that some kind of frigging trick question? How the fuck do you think I felt?"

"Language, Randall. Any more, and you'll go back to your cell," the prison officer warned gruffly.

"Take me back. I'd rather be there than listen to this shit!" he retorted, glancing over his shoulder at the officer.

Undeterred, Sally pressed, "I'm sorry. It was a simple question. Maybe I should have rephrased it."

"Maybe you should have. Better still, maybe you shouldn't have asked the damn question in the first effing place. She was my kid, my own flesh and blood. How the hell do you think I felt? I was devastated." He pointed at Sally. "And what frigging use were your lot? Eh? Useless, that's what you were. A little kiddie dies, and you stop investigating the case after a few weeks. Work that one out if you can, because I couldn't at the time. And here you are now, what, twenty-odd years later to open up old wounds? It's nuts, that's what it is. Why? Why have you opened the case up again?"

Sally sighed. She understood the man being so angry; she was feeling some of that anger herself because of Falkirk's screw-up.

"There are reasons why we're now looking into the case, things I'm not prepared to go into."

"Why? You think I'm stupid or something? You lot messed up, royally messed up, and now you're trying to make amends for your mistakes."

Sally exhaled a deep breath. "I hate to admit it, but yes, you're right. The initial police investigation wasn't thorough enough."

"Hallelujah! A copper who admits when she is in the wrong."

"Except I wasn't in the wrong. I wasn't even a serving officer at the time of the murder, so please don't hold that against me. I'm doing my best to put things right here, so I'd appreciate you giving me some slack."

"What? Instead of enough rope to hang yourself? You lot are a bloody waste of space. Every time I committed a crime, I handed myself in. Knew your lot wouldn't have the brains to figure out it was me committing the crimes. I'd never kill someone, though, I draw the line there. All my wrongdoings were against property."

"Aren't you forgetting the ABH charge?"

He scratched the stubble on his chin. "Well, what are you supposed to do when someone you were on a job with starts messing you about? I slapped him around a bit. He was embarrassed and battered me with the charge of ABH, fecking idiot. Still, I'm grateful for one thing."

"What's that?"

"It earned me a longer stretch in here." He laughed and leaned back.

Sally tutted. "Getting back to the investigation. Your son told the officer in charge of the case that an intruder entered the house."

"Yep, that's what I heard, too, and?"

"Someone in your line of business…"

He held a hand up. "No way. I'm gonna stop you right there, lady. I've already told you that none of my crimes involved hurting anyone. So, you're wrong, it wasn't someone in *my line of business*. Let's get things right here, okay?"

"Okay, it was a slip of the tongue on my part. Let's say that a burglar broke in and things went awry on the night."

"I don't get that. I'm a 'professional burglar', if you like. I still maintain that I wouldn't kill anyone on a job, let alone a frigging six-year-old who was asleep in her bed."

"I see. Over the years, during your stay in prison, have you heard a whisper about a possible name perhaps?"

"Are you kidding me? Is someone likely to walk up to me and tell me they murdered my kid?"

"I didn't say that. Please don't twist my words, Seb. We all know that gossip filters the corridors of these places. I just wondered if anything about your daughter's murder had come your way."

"And if it had, I would have killed the son of a bitch who did the deed. Any father would tell you the same thing."

"Okay, I'm sorry if my question caused you any offence. I'm simply searching for another angle in which to take the case forward."

"Look all you want. I wasn't there that night, neither was that damn ex of mine. She's responsible for Millie's death, no one else."

"I understand how upset you probably were when you heard the news…"

"Lady, you have no idea. That child was as precious to me as she was to my ex. She kept the kids from me."

"I'm sorry to hear that; however, as I was saying, I don't think you can blame Millie's death on Anna. She was entitled to a life of her own and she left the children in the capable hands of a babysitter. Unfortunately, a family emergency cropped up which meant the children were alone for a short time. That bad luck could have happened to anyone."

"Bad luck! Are you for frigging real? Would you call your child being murdered bad luck?"

"I didn't say that. Of course I wouldn't phrase such a vile incident in that way. I was referring to the circumstances that occurred that evening. I do wish you'd stop twisting my words, Mr Randall."

His gaze dropped to the table, and he wrung his hands together. Sally could tell he was getting agitated.

"Okay, I think we'll leave it there. I'm sorry if coming here today has brought back any bad memories you've had to deal with over the years."

He glanced up, his blue eyes swimming with tears. "You have no idea what pain I've had to deal with. Promise me you'll find the bastard who did this. He's been at large far too long as it is."

"I can't make you a promise because of the time issue. For all we know, the perpetrator could be dead by now, but what I can do is give you the assurance that the case will be fully investigated by me and my team. Thank you for agreeing to see us today."

Sally and Jack left the room.

"That was sad," Jack said quietly as they strode up the corridor back to the reception area.

"Very. It actually chipped away at my heart. The man clearly let his family down big time, but there is no doubt in my mind how much he loved that child. I'm pretty sure we can discount him from our enquiries."

"I'm inclined to agree with you."

They reached a junction of corridors. There were a few prisoners standing next to the bars just chatting. Sally kept her head down, not wishing to make eye contact with any of them, knowing how some prisoners got off on intimidating female visitors.

"There she is, the bitch who got Darryl transferred," one of the men said, his tone aggressive in nature.

"Keep walking," Jack suggested. "Ignore them."

Ha! Easier said than done, matey.

"Not a bad looker, though. Wouldn't mind meeting her down a dark alley and showing her a good time," one of the other men shouted after them.

Sally hesitated for a second or two, but Jack tugged on her arm, urged her to keep walking. Up ahead of them, two prison officers were watching what was going on. One of them gestured for Sally and Jack to keep moving. That was what they did.

Anger bubbled up inside her, and her cheeks heated up. She sensed the bars closing in on her and was desperate to get out in the fresh air.

Moments later, she took in a gulp of clean air and leaned against the wall outside the reception area, staring across the car park. "Jesus, my heart is racing. I was determined not to respond to their taunting; it was so frigging difficult for me."

Jack rubbed her back. "You did well. If the bars hadn't been between us, I would have throttled each and every one of those bastards for doing that to you. Arseholes. Maybe you should reconsider any future visits."

Sally stood upright and thrust her shoulders back. "And let them win? Not on your nelly. I'm getting stronger every day, thanks to having a loving man in my life. I'll continue to grow and come back here one day and wipe the floor with those guys. Darryl is still trying to disrupt my life even though he's over two hundred miles away. I'm determined not to let him do that. Thanks for your support, Jack, it means a lot to me."

"You'll always have that, Sally. And yes, you're right, you're growing stronger by the day. Everyone has noticed that at work. We're right behind you, you know that. The bastard can no longer hurt you, either physically or mentally, take heart from that."

"Thanks, Jack. I know you're right." She tapped a pointed finger at her temple. "It's the crap dwelling up here that is proving to be a bugger to shift. I'll get there eventually. He definitely did a number on me. I know I'm safe now, but there's going to come a time when he'll be walking the streets again. That's when I sense my life will be turned upside down."

"The prison will keep you informed about when he's up for parole. That'll give you a heads-up about the future, won't it?"

She placed her hand over her pounding heart. "But in here, I just know that I haven't heard the last of him. Not only that, I've brought Simon into the equation now, put his life in jeopardy, if you will. Please don't tell me I'm thinking irrationally about this."

Jack hooked his arm through hers, encouraging her towards the car. He didn't speak again until they were inside the vehicle. "I wouldn't dream of telling you that you're being irrational after what that fecker put you through. What I need you to understand is that there are people around you who love you and would bend over backwards, break the law if they have to, to ensure your safety. Got that?"

She turned and smiled at him, then placed a hand over his. "Thank you, I appreciate that more than you know. The last thing I want, however, would be for any of you to lose your jobs because of him. Let's not waste any more breath on the bastard. Let's get back to the station."

"Agreed. If anything should crop up in the future, we'll deal with it then."

They punched fists.

"Deal."

Ten minutes from the station, Sally's mobile rang. She beamed when she saw who the call was from. "Hello, Lorne, I was thinking about you last night. Are you all settled now?"

Lorne Warner let out a crazed laugh. "Hardly, but we're getting there. How are you?"

Sally shrugged, even though Lorne wasn't there to see her do it. "I'm fine. Just been to the prison to see an inmate about a new case we've opened up."

"Shit! How did that go? Are you all right? I know how much you hate going to that place."

"So-so. There was an uncomfortable incident, but my brilliant partner, Jack, helped me overcome it. Enough about me. When do you think you'll be up to having visitors?"

"As long as you're sure you're okay, no matter how busy I am, you know I'm always here for you."

"Thanks, you're an amazing friend, Lorne."

"How about coming over for a barbecue this weekend? We're celebrating after discovering the boxes with all the plates in." Lorne laughed.

"What do you mean?"

"Nothing, a family joke." She lowered her voice to add, "Someone forgot to write on the boxes what the contents were."

"Oh heck, seriously? That someone being your darling husband, I take it?"

"Bingo! Bless him. Maybe it was payback for landing him with the onerous chore in the first place, I don't know. You've got the address?"

"I have. What time shall we come over? Oops, I take it Simon is invited, too."

Lorne chuckled. "Of course he is, as long as he's not one of these pathologists who is keen on pointing out what part of an animal we're eating."

Sally chuckled, her heart so much lighter now that she was speaking to one of her dearest friends. "Nope, he's well-behaved in that department. We'll bring a few bottles of wine with us. Anything else? Can I tempt you with a shop-bought salted caramel cheesecake I've just discovered at Tesco's? It's lush."

"Sounds perfect to round off a meat-laden barbecue. See you around twelve on Sunday then?"

"Can't wait to see you both again. I know it's only been a few months since our wedding, but it seems a lifetime ago. Have I told you how excited I am to have you living close by?"

"Not lately. We're super excited to be here, not that we've ventured out much since our arrival. Hopefully the last of the boxes will be sorted by the time you come."

"Relax, don't work too hard for our benefit."

"You might regret saying that, we're both knackered."

"Are you sure you want us to come this weekend then?"

"Definitely. See you Sunday."

"Okay. Love to both of you." Sally ended the call, aware of the soppy grin she had fixed in place.

"It'll be nice having her living close to you. Maybe she can drop by the station now and again," Jack said.

"Maybe. I know how much you admire her and her work ethic."

"What's not to admire? She was one of the Met's finest coppers."

"Does Donna know about this infatuation you have?"

"What? Bloody hell, don't even joke about things like that. She'd string me up if she thought I was keen on another woman. I was talking professionally. Any serving officer would feel the same way as I do about your best buddy, wouldn't they?"

Sally turned and raised her eyebrows at him. "You keep telling yourself that, matey. Good luck if Donna ever finds out. I hope you don't have a tree in your back garden."

She laughed as the colour drained from his face.

"Jesus, remind me not to show you any sympathy in the future if you turn the tables on me like this."

She punched his arm. "I'm winding you up, Bullet, lighten up. Maybe you're onto something, though. I mean about trying to persuade Lorne to visit us at the station. She's got an amazing gut reaction to cases that very few of us possess. If we're truly stuck on a case, perhaps she could be persuaded to take a look at it for us."

"DCI Green would have a field day with that. He'd probably pull you up on it, too, condemning you for using an outside source, and that in turn would make him doubt your abilities. Is that what you want?"

"Ugh…you might have a point there. It wouldn't take much for him to think that. He's an odd one at the best of times. Maybe we'll put that idea on hold for now."

They continued the rest of the journey listening to the radio.

They breezed through the station and into the incident room to find the other team members busy at their computers.

"We'll just grab a coffee and then fill you in on what we learned today," Sally announced, heading towards the vending machine. After depositing Jack's coffee, she perched on the desk closest to Joanna.

She ran through the reception they'd received from Seb Randall and told the rest of the team how upset he still was about his daughter's death."

"Do you think that's why he's a serial offender?" Joanna asked. "Are you saying he feels secure in there, rather than facing up to things in the outside world?"

"I reckon so. It's a sad reality when someone fails to come to terms with a tragedy such as a child's death. Understandable, though, in some cases. Sitting there staring at the bars all day would drive me nuts and make me consider my life more. I don't know, each to their own, I guess."

"I'm with you. At least on the outside you'd be able to immerse yourself in some form of distraction, like a hobby or something along those lines," Joanna agreed.

"Anyway, I've come to the conclusion that he had nothing whatsoever to do with his daughter's death. Although, he didn't once talk positively about his ex, but then who does?"

Joanna tapped her cheek with her pen. "Should we discount him, though? What if he wanted to take his revenge for his ex out on the child? Is that even feasible?"

"Maybe we'll keep him on the substitutes list for now. He could have been pulling a fast one on me and Jack. Who bloody knows with these prisoners? Most of them set out to mess up an investigation anyway. I must say, in this case, I got the impression he was genuine enough."

"I agree," Jack shouted across the room.

The phone rang on Joanna's desk. She answered it and handed the phone to Sally and mouthed, "It's Louie Pickrel."

Sally nodded. "Hello, Mr Pickrel."

"Are you the officer I should speak to regarding my sister's case?"

"That's right. Detective Inspector Sally Parker. When would it be convenient to have a chat with you, sir? Your mother mentioned you're on the road a fair bit."

"I am. I have a day off booked in a few days. I have a dentist appointment in the afternoon but I could squeeze you in during the morning, if that suits you?"

"Wonderful. What day?"

"Thursday. Where? At my house or the station?"

"My partner and I can come out to see you if it's more convenient."

"Fine. My address is sixty-three Fordacre Road, Acle. Just around the corner from my mother. Do you know it?"

"We'll find it, don't worry. Shall we say ten o'clock?"

"That suits me. I'll see you then. Goodbye, Inspector."

"Goodbye, sir."

Sally pulled a face. "Not sure how to read him from that phone call. He was very business-like. Sounded as though he was talking to a client."

"Professionals have a tendency to be like that," Jack suggested.

"Okay. Make a note of that appointment for me, Joanna, if you would. Thursday at ten, sixty-three Fordacre Road, Acle. I'm intrigued to hear what he has to say. I hope he remembers clearly the events of what took place that night. I've dealt with people in the past who were children at the time a crime was committed, and their memories have been a touch sketchy. Hopefully, Louie Pickrel will be as efficient as his manner. Right, back to the here and now. Where are we with regard to tracing the babysitter and the neighbours?"

"I have a couple of the neighbours. I've arranged to pay them a visit. If you're too busy, I don't mind going out to interview them," Joanna replied.

"When have you arranged to see them?"

"Tomorrow."

"In that case, Jack and I will do it unless anything else crops up in the meantime. Have you checked into their backgrounds?"

"I'm in the process of going through that now."

"Good, get as much information as you can for us today. If there's anything suspicious, we can hit them with it when we visit them. The babysitter?"

Joanna nodded. "I contacted Lisa this morning. She was reluctant to agree to a visit, but I wore her down eventually. I slotted her in for four this afternoon. I hope I did the right thing, boss."

"Of course you did. The sooner we get these interviews out of the way the better. Right, I'm going to spend the next few hours in my office going over the file. I want to ensure I touch base on everything before I reinterview these people."

"What do you want the rest of us to do?" Jack asked.

"Keep doing the background checks. Find out how long the Pickrels lived at that address. It's possible we could be dealing with a mistaken identity. Highly unlikely, but you never know. Also, I'd like someone to search the archives for similar crimes in the area around that time."

"I can do that," Stuart volunteered.

"Good. Search before and after the crime date, Stuart."

"How long either side, boss?"

"Why don't we go for a couple of years?"

"Wow, okay, I was thinking a couple of months. Leave it with me, I'll see what I can do."

"Rightio. I'm going to give this case until the end of the week with all of us working on it. If we draw a blank, then I'm going to suggest splitting up the team and starting another case. How does that sound to you guys?"

Jack nodded. "Sounds fair enough to me."

The rest of the team agreed and got on with their work. Sally went through to her office and spent the next few hours going over the slim file and making notes. The E-FIT of a man sat prominently in front of her. He looked like any other regular guy, no distinguishing features. No bushy eyebrows that met in the middle that her gran always used to say signified a killer on the streets. Nothing. Studying the picture, she could understand why Falkirk hadn't shown it to the press, or could she? She was in two minds about that one.

An idea struck her. She rang one of her many contacts for help. "Phil Edmunds. How can I help?"

"Hey, you, it's Sally Parker. How's it going?"

"Quiet, in desperate need of a juicy murder story to boost my salary. As it stands, no bonus on the cards for me for the first time in months. How are things with you, Sally? Still working the cold cases that arsehole screwed up?"

Sally sniggered. Phil wasn't the type to mince his words, he never had been. He was an excellent journalist, one she could trust with her life if it came to the crunch. He'd helped her out on a few cases in the past. They had an understanding, one that worked both ways sometimes. Not too often in Sally's direction, though. "Unfortunately. Can you spare me a few minutes of your valuable time?"

It was a genuine question, but Phil laughed anyway. "You're a scream. Shoot. What do you need from me?"

"If I mentioned the name Todd Stockard, would it ring a bell?"

"Ha! I ain't Quasimodo." He laughed again.

"Sorry, that one flew right over my head. Did you crack a funny?"

"Obviously not. Shall we forget I said anything? Todd Stockard, you say. Yes, I remember him. He left here about ten years ago. The boss got fed up of him overstepping the mark all the time. One warning too many. In the end, he suffered the terminal chop."

"Damn. Any idea where he is now? What county he's in?"

"Still in Norfolk last I heard. I think he gave up being a journalist and became a novelist. Tough job that, not sure I could make the transition."

"Wow, okay. Writing fiction or non-fiction?"

"Now you're testing my memory. Let me do a quick Google search for you." He tapped on his computer and supplied her with the answer within a few seconds. "Here you go. He writes under the name of T G Stockard and, well, bugger me, he writes non-fiction. Actually, you two would probably get on like a house on fire."

Sally frowned. "Meaning?"

"Meaning that he delves into unsolved cases and highlights them in his books."

"Interesting. I'll see if my team can track him down. Thanks, Phil."

"Whoa! You can't leave me hanging like that. What's he supposed to have done wrong?"

"Sorry. We've opened up a new case, a cold case going back nineteen years. I've heard from the mother that he caused a problem at the funeral, went against the family's wishes and photographed the child's coffin in the grave."

"Jesus, what an absolute tosser."

"Agreed. I just wanted to track him down to ask him a few questions, that's all. We're struggling with this case and we've only just begun. It would be good to get some kind of insight from him about it if he was around back then."

"Good idea. Sorry you've been handed another tough case. Give me a shout if you need a hand with anything."

"Actually, now you've mentioned it, I could do with an insider to tell me how this case went down via the media, if you're up to digging into it for me?"

"For you, anything. Want to leave it with me for a day or two?"

"Don't you want to know what case it is?"

"Oops…I forgot that part. My pen is at the ready."

Sally tutted. "What are you like? It's the Millie Pickrel case. She was six when she was murdered in her own home by an intruder."

"Damn. That's a tough one to swallow for the parents. Were they in the house?"

"Nope. The father was banged up in a prison cell. The brother, who was twelve at the time, was at home and disturbed the killer. He called nine-nine-nine and was trying his best to revive her when the paramedics got there."

"Shit, the poor kid, or should I say kids? And the mother? Don't tell me she was the irresponsible type who went out and left her kids to fend for themselves at night?"

"No. She was out on her first date in years, arranged for a babysitter to look after the kids, but the girl learned of an emergency and had to leave. The babysitter's father died of a heart attack that night as well."

"Holy crap, are you kidding me?"

"I wish I was. It's all true."

"Okay, I'll see what I can find out and get back to you later on today. If I get snowed under, can I ring you when you're off duty this evening?"

"Of course you can. You don't usually ask my permission."

"You weren't married then. Congratulations, by the way."

Her cheeks warmed up, and she smiled. "Idiot. Thanks. Simon is cool, unlike my previous husband."

"Glad you've found a decent man at last, Sally, you deserve to be happy, love."

"You're too kind. I've gotta go. I have something in my eye that needs my attention."

"You daft mare. Okay, be in touch soon."

"Thanks, matey. Nice chatting to you."

"Ditto," Phil said then hung up.

Jack must have been standing on the other side of the door listening, because as soon as she placed the phone in its docking station, he entered the room. "How's it going? Brushed up on the case yet?"

"Sort of. Just got off the phone to my journalist friend. He's going to look back in the archives for me. You know that journalist who spoilt the funeral for the family? He's now an author."

"Really? I bet he's raking it in."

"Not necessarily. I've heard that some authors just write to free their minds of all the clutter jumbled up in their heads. Here's a staggering statistic for you to devour: most UK authors barely manage to scrape together the minimum wage, can you believe that?"

"How do you know that?"

"I read an article about it the other day, somewhere. I also read that there's a relatively new craze of people self-publishing rather than going through a traditional publisher."

"Who'd have thunk it? I bet that ticks the publishers off."

"Maybe. It's their loss if these guys go on to be successful."

"True. Right, what's on the agenda?"

"Now I've had a good look at things, I think our next stop should be the babysitter. Have you got her address handy?"

He waved a sheet of paper in his right hand and offered her a smug grin. "Thought you might say that."

"Let's go then."

4

Lisa Watson opened the door to her terraced home. She looked around thirty-five. Her hair had blonde highlights with purple streaks running through it. Lisa welcomed them and showed them into the lounge. "Take a seat."

"Thanks, Lisa. I should formally introduce myself to you. I'm DI Sally Parker, and this big guy is my partner, DS Jack Blackman. Try not to be worried, you're not in any trouble, we're only here to ascertain all the facts."

"Why now? Why have you reopened the case after all this time? It doesn't make sense." She was sitting on a beanbag she'd pulled from the corner of the room while Sally and Jack sat on the fabric-covered two-seater couch. The room wasn't really big enough for any further furniture apart from a small cabinet which housed a thirty-inch TV along one of the walls. It was a cosy room, painted in a soft green hue.

"Two reasons. One is that as a cold case team we've been tasked to check a few cases yet unsolved in our area, and the second reason is because we're approaching the twenty-year anniversary of this heinous crime. The family have been crying out for answers for years, and no one has listened to them. We're here to make up for that and to try and bring the culprit to justice. Our ultimate aim is to give Anna the closure she needs to move on with her life."

"Move on with her life? She's remarried, hasn't she? And had another child from what I've heard. I'd say she has moved on all right." Her hands shook in her lap. She was clenching them together to prevent them from trembling out of control from what Sally could tell.

"Do I detect a note of bitterness in your tone, Lisa?" Sally asked, sitting on the edge of the uncomfortable couch.

"Yes and no. I'm happy she's moved on. Some of us haven't been as fortunate as her."

"Meaning you?"

"Yes, me. Two people were lost that night, and I've never forgiven myself for the part I played in their deaths."

"You blame yourself? Why? From what I recollect about the case, no blame was ever laid at your door."

"It should have been. I should never have left the kids alone that night. I was in charge of them. If it hadn't been for that call from my mum, well, I would have stayed at the house and I could have fought off the intruder."

"And you might not be here today," Sally replied, feeling sorry for the woman and the obvious torture she'd subjected herself to over the years.

"At least I would have gone down fighting. Millie didn't stand a chance. She was an adorable child. Her laughter filled that house. Even if you weren't in the same room as her you could hear her treasured laugh." She ran a shaking hand over her face, and her eyes swelled with unshed tears.

"No one could have predicted how things would turn out."

"I shouldn't have left the children alone."

Sally shook her head. "I think you're wrong. Any other decent human being in your position would have done the same thing."

"Would they? I doubt it. The least I could have done was ask a neighbour to sit with the children while Anna was on her way back. I *didn't*. Knowing that has haunted me day and night ever since."

"You've punished yourself unnecessarily over the years then,

Goodbye My Precious child

Lisa. What were you at the time? Sixteen? I know where my head would have been at that age, with my own family. No one could've known what would happen in your absence. It was an unfortunate incident, made far worse by the fact that you lost your own father that night."

The tears trickled down her cheeks, and Lisa swiped them away. "I'll never rid myself of this feeling, ever."

"Why? Why do you persist in punishing yourself like this?"

"I deserve to be punished for failing Anna. She put her trust in me to look after those children, and what did I do? I ran out on them, leaving them in a perilous position."

Sally's heart went out to the young woman who had been riddled with guilt for the past nineteen years. "You had other priorities, Lisa."

"Dad was already dead by the time I got to the hospital…I was too late to say goodbye to him."

The sobs came then and continued for the next five to ten minutes. In that time, Sally instructed Jack to make them a drink. She knelt on the floor beside Lisa and placed a soothing hand on the woman's back, rubbing it gently up and down her spine.

"I'm so sorry, not only for your devastating loss but for the guilt you've unnecessarily carried on your shoulders all these years."

Lisa wiped her nose on the sleeve of her cardigan. "There's no need for you to feel sorry for me. It's Millie you should feel sorry for, Millie and Anna, oh, and Louie, of course. What that child must have gone through that night is nobody's business. I haven't seen him since Millie's funeral; he could barely look at me at the graveside. I know he blamed me for leaving them. I tried to speak to him that day, to apologise, but he hid behind his mother and refused to talk to me. My father's funeral happened the same day, by the way. I made sure I attended both funerals because of the guilt factor."

"That was kind of you. All I can say is that Louie's own feelings must have been in turmoil at the time. I'm sure he didn't mean to blank you. Twelve-year-olds must be a handful to deal with at the best of times."

She shook her head. "I don't think he was. He was a loving child who thought the world of his sister, and she was no longer around because of the mistake I made."

Jack entered the room with a tray of mugs. He held out a black coffee to Lisa. She accepted it with a weak smile of appreciation.

"Thanks, Jack." Sally took a second mug off the tray.

"Do you want me to leave the room?" he asked.

Sally smiled. "Would you mind?"

He nodded, took the tray with him and closed the door gently behind him.

Sally retook her seat on the couch and cradled her mug in both hands. "I know how difficult this must be for you, Lisa, and I'm sorry if my being here is stirring up old memories you'd rather forget, but I have to ask if you saw anything out of the ordinary that night."

Lisa shook her head. "It's not stirring up the memories because they're constantly with me, twenty-four hours a day. I wish I could rid myself of them. It's impossible."

"Have you considered counselling?"

"I've seen several shrinks over the years. They've all assured me I wasn't to blame for what happened, but deep down, I know that's not true."

"I can't pretend to know what you're going through. As an outsider, all I can do is point out that no one could have dreamt anything like this would have happened while you were watching the children. Do you really think Anna would have employed you if she'd sensed things were going to go wrong? No, she wouldn't. Please, you must stop the guilt eating away at you. What job do you do, Lisa?"

"I don't work. I've tried to hold down a number of jobs over the years but I've only lasted a few days."

"You have some serious issues which need addressing before you search for another job. How long do you think you can go on like this?"

"As long as it takes. I know how foolish I'm being. What you don't understand is that every time I close my eyes, I see Millie's precious smiling face. How do you suggest I rid myself of that? It's not even as if my father's face appears; the guilt of not saying goodbye to him that evening pales into insignificance compared to the guilt I feel for leaving Millie. Surely you can understand how I must feel?"

Sally shook her head. "Not really. There's the old adage that time is a great healer. Let it heal you, love. If you don't do it soon, then I fear you're going to end up in an early grave."

Lisa raised her head to look at Sally. "I know. I hope it happens soon."

Sally gasped. "You don't mean that?"

"I do. Over the years, when things have got on top of me, I've attempted to end my life."

Tears pricked Sally's eyes. "That's tough, I'm sorry you feel that way. You've wasted your whole adult life with the guilt you carry with you. You have to move on, Lisa. Don't be a prisoner to your emotions."

"I wish that intruder had killed me instead of that beautiful, innocent child. I can't emphasise that enough. She was a cherished little girl, cherished by her mother and brother and me, a complete stranger…I let them down."

Sally sensed no matter what she said to the woman, Lisa wasn't about to listen to her. She sipped her drink instead as the room fell silent. After a while, she asked, "When you left the property that night, did you see anyone on the street?"

"No, not that I can remember. He must have been there, loitering in the shadows, waiting for me to leave the house. If I'd seen anyone, I would've reconsidered my position and gone back inside the house and locked the door. There was no one around."

"Okay, well, if there's nothing else you can help me with, then I'm going to leave. However, I'm concerned about your well-being. I don't feel inclined to leave you when your heart is breaking like this. Is there anyone I can call, your mother perhaps?"

"No. Mum and I lost contact with each other a few years ago. She can't understand me punishing myself over a *mere child*—her words not mine."

"Oh dear, that's a shame. Do you have any siblings?"

"No, I'm an only child. I'll be fine, Inspector. Please don't worry about me. What happens now, with regard to the investigation?"

"We've had to start from scratch, which is tough almost twenty years later. Over the coming weeks we'll be interviewing everyone who made a statement at the time, searching for clues that were possibly missed during the initial investigation. If I leave you a card, will you promise to ring me if you think of anything I should know about? My visit might jolt a memory once I've gone."

"I doubt it. I'll get in touch if anything comes to mind. Do you think it's possible that the intruder did this to other families? Robbed them of their children?"

"That's another angle we're pursuing at present. Most burglaries are just that. These people tend to go after valuable possessions. It's extremely rare that an intruder breaks into a house with the intention of killing someone, let alone a small child."

"I read that at the time. Do you think that's why the investigation didn't really get off the ground?"

Sally hitched up her right shoulder. "Who knows?"

Lisa gasped. "What if this person is dead? What happens then?"

"Then there's very little we can do about it. All that will do is give the family the peace of mind that the person concerned can no longer hurt anyone."

"I hope he isn't. He deserves to be put away for the rest of his life. And when you find the culprit, please make sure the other prisoners know what he is guilty of. Maybe the prisoners will mete out their own punishment."

"Prisoners have a tendency to be aware of what goes on in the outside world, so I doubt the news of any likely arrest will remain a secret for long. God help him if that happens. I know I'm going over old ground here, but please, Lisa, promise me you'll seek help when I go?"

"I can't promise that, Inspector. I wish you luck with the investigation."

They both stood.

Sally hugged Lisa. "Ditto, Lisa. You're a special lady who doesn't deserve to punish herself like this."

"Thank you, but in all honesty, you don't know me."

Sally winked. "I'm a good judge of character…most of the time," she added after a slight pause as Darryl's face entered her mind. She quickly pushed the abhorrent image aside and returned to the front door with Lisa. Jack was waiting just outside the front door. "Here's my card. Ring me if you remember anything you want to add or if you need my help with anything."

"Thank you, I will."

"I mean it. If ever you feel the need to reach out to someone, I can help, okay?"

Lisa placed a hand halfway up the door and leaned her head against it. "I appreciate it, Inspector. Good luck."

Sally smiled and walked back to Jack's car. They both got inside.

Sally heaved out a large sigh and stared back to see Lisa closing the door. "Can you imagine the heartache that young woman has been through over the years?"

"Self-inflicted by the sounds of it. The mother didn't blame her, did she?"

"No, that's true. What a shame. All those years wasted. Who's to say what amount of torment still lies ahead of her in the future?" Sally reflected, saddened for the young woman.

"Back to base?"

"Yep, I think so."

Upon their return, they discovered the rest of the team had gone above and beyond to locate nearly all of the Pickrels' immediate neighbours. Joanna eagerly passed over a sheet of paper for Sally to peruse during her cup of coffee at her desk. Jack joined her in the office.

"Are we going to interview these people or pass it over to the team?"

"Is that what you think we should do?"

He shrugged. "I don't care."

"Wait a minute," Sally said, glancing down at the sheet.

"Go on, don't keep me waiting. What's up?"

"One of the neighbours has got a rap sheet for indecent assault on a child."

Jack's eyes widened. "Shit. Is that recent? Or was it around the time of the murder?"

"He went to prison after the murder." She tapped the paper with her finger. "Now that's interesting, right?"

"Very. Where is he now? In or out?"

"Looks like he's out at present. I think we should pay him a visit, don't you?"

Jack nodded, shrugged and swigged the rest of his coffee. "Here we go again."

"I like to keep you on your toes, big man. It's the highlight of my day."

"You do that all right. I wouldn't mind having a day at my desk now and again. You know, to recharge the batteries, instead of gallivanting all over the county."

Sally finished her drink and left her desk. "Stop your whinging. If you need a rest, I'll drive. I can't be any fairer than that."

"Big deal. Okay, you're on. I might have forty winks on the way."

Sally raised an eyebrow. "Over my dead body, Sergeant Blackman."

He pulled a face. "I've worked for more appreciative bosses in the past."

Sally placed a hand near her mouth and whispered, "Bullshit."

"I heard that," he grumbled, following her out of the office.

"We're off out, gang. Keep digging. Well done on finding this out, Joanna." Sally waved the sheet at her.

"Damn. I don't know what's wrong with me. I knew there was something important on there I should have pointed out to you. Sorry, boss."

Sally approached her desk. "It's unlike you, Jo. Anything wrong?"

"Family problems on my mind. I'll try and not let them interfere in the future."

Sally lowered her voice and asked, "Anything you want to discuss?"

"It'll work itself out, boss. Thanks for asking, though. Sorry to have let you down."

"Let's get one thing straight, Constable, you have *never* let me down, nor are you likely to in the future." Sally smiled and held up her crossed fingers.

"I'll make sure I don't." Joanna gave her a glimmer of a smile that did nothing to shift the worrying frown from the constable's face.

"We can have a chat later, if you need one."

"I'll think about it."

Sally nodded and joined Jack at the door.

"Don't forget your promise, you're driving." He grinned.

She rolled her eyes and patted the keys in her jacket pocket. "As if I don't do enough bloody work around here as it is."

She walked down the stairs ahead of him and heard him chuckling behind her. She turned quickly to glare at him.

"Where's your sense of humour gone?"

"On strike."

"Tell me something I don't know," he grumbled.

It took them twenty-five minutes to drive out to the estate where the murder had taken place nineteen years earlier.

"This is it. It's derelict by the look of things." Jack pointed to a small terraced house that had fallen into disrepair.

"Hardly surprising given that a child died there. Who'd choose to live there?" Sally swallowed down the saliva filling her mouth.

"That's the house we need, next door."

Sally switched off the engine, and they both got out of the car and made their way up the short concrete path to the front door. The garden was covered in slate with the odd shrub placed here and there. A low-maintenance garden if ever she saw one. To her, it had a woman's touch about it. Was Stanton married? Joanna hadn't provided her with that information. She would need to tread carefully if he was. *Sod it! No, I don't. If he hasn't told his wife about his past, that's his problem, not mine.*

Jack did the honours of ringing the doorbell. They both withdrew their warrant cards ready to show the occupants.

A brunette woman in her forties or fifties opened the door a mere six inches and peered around it. "Can I help you?"

Sally thrust her card towards the woman, and the woman gasped.

"I'm DI Sally Parker, and this is my partner, DS Jack Blackman. Are you Mrs Stanton?"

"No. There is no Mrs Stanton."

"I see. Who are you then?"

"A friend of Roger's. What do you want?"

"To speak with Roger. Is he at home?"

"Umm…yes. Er…it's not convenient right now."

Oh crap! Don't tell me they were in the middle of an afternoon frigging romp! "Sorry if we've interrupted anything, but our visit is extremely important. We'll give you five minutes to get dressed, if that's what you want."

The woman's pale face reddened with a blush. "Very well."

She shut the door and left them shuffling their feet on the doorstep.

"Don't tell me they were bloody at it at this time of the day." Jack groaned under his breath.

"I know. I feel physically sick and I haven't even met the man yet."

"Me, too. I suppose we have to be thankful the sun is shining and it's not raining."

"True enough."

It was another few minutes before the man they'd come to see opened the door to greet them. Well, perhaps greet was a bit of a stretch. "The filth? What brings you to my bloody door? Don't you lot know what an appointment is? People have a damn life to lead, you know," he shouted without taking a breath.

"Want to calm down there, mate?" Jack tried to placate the irate man.

Stanton ran a hand through his short grey hair once he realised Jack meant business. "Sorry. What's this about? I've had my share of you lot over the years."

"We're making general enquiries, sir, that's all. Would it be okay if we came in for a while?"

"Get inside quick, I don't want the neighbours knowing you lot are here." He opened the door wide to allow them access.

The woman who had spoken to them a few moments earlier was coming down the stairs, tucking a T-shirt into her trousers. "Do you want a drink? I'm making one anyway."

Stanton shot her a warning glance. She lowered her gaze, embarrassed.

"We're fine. We don't want to outstay our welcome. Are you free to speak with us, Mr Stanton?"

"In here. I can spare you five minutes, that's all."

He showed them into a medium-sized tidy lounge that contained two leather sofas and an enormous TV screen.

"Take a seat, if you must. Don't get too comfortable, though."

"We get your drift that you're not keen on seeing us, Mr Stanton. You haven't done anything wrong, or have you?"

He held his arms out to the sides. "If I knew what this was about, maybe I'd be able to answer you."

"We're investigating a case that happened nineteen years ago."

He turned to look out of the front window, shook his head and said, "Jesus!"

"Ah, you're aware of the case then?"

He faced Sally again. "Of course I'm bloody aware of it. If you've come here to pin that murder on me, then I'm telling you now, you'll be ruddy wasting your time."

"You were living here at the time of the murder, yes?"

"You know damn well I was."

"Why the animosity?" Sally asked, peering into his eyes.

His gaze dropped from hers, and his hands clenched and unclenched in his lap. "How would you feel? Yes, I've done wrong in the past. I was punished for that. I didn't do nothing to that kid, though. Not sure how many times I have to tell you lot that."

"You were questioned at the time?"

"Of course I was. We all were. I can't believe you've reopened the case. Why now?"

"We have our reasons that I'm not prepared to disclose at the moment."

"You have your reasons? That's right, it doesn't take much for you bastards to come chasing innocent folks down, does it?" He punched the arm of the sofa.

"You'd be advised to tone down that temper of yours, mate," Jack warned, leaping to Sally's defence.

"As I've already stated, we're not singling you out in this, sir. We're here to question again everyone who was living in the area at the time. The family deserve to know what happened to Millie, surely you can understand that?"

He sighed heavily, his chest expanding. "All right, I suppose I get that. But you have to believe me when I tell you I had nothing to do with that kiddie's death. None of us did around here. We were as shocked as you guys were. Most of us joined in the search for the suspect once we saw that E-FIT."

"You saw the E-FIT? Did you recognise the man?"

"I did, and if I'd recognised him then, I'm sure I would have told your lot at the time and an arrest would have been made."

His tone had turned sarcastic. Jack cleared his throat, encouraging the man to look his way. He wagged a warning finger at him.

"Sorry," Stanton muttered. "You lot make me feel uncomfortable in my own home."

"It's not our fault you feel that way. Maybe if you hadn't broken the law in the past you wouldn't feel uncomfortable," Jack replied.

"All right, there's no need to keep shoving it down my neck. What I did was a one-off. In case you're not aware of the full facts, the girl I had sex with—yes, it was consensual sex, I don't care what she said in court—she lied. Just like when she told me she was sixteen when we fell into bed after a drunken night out. She was bloody thirteen, the lying bitch. You know she turned round and tried to blackmail me, don't you?"

"No, I wasn't aware of the full facts of your case, sir."

"And that's where the frigging problem lies. No one cares about the facts, it's someone's record that defines their future, isn't it?"

"Perhaps that's true. Okay, going back to the crime of the murder. Did you know the family?"

"Sort of. Only to wave at now and again. I tended to keep myself to myself back then."

"May I ask why?"

He shrugged. "It's a free country as far as I know, I could do what I like."

Jack shook his head. "Don't start, mate. Play nicely."

"It's okay, Jack, it's obvious Mr Stanton has a problem with authority."

"Do I fuck? It's you lot I've got the problem with. Do you realise how many innocent blokes there are sitting in our prisons? I met a fair few in my time there. It's sickening. Most of them have been stitched up by coppers, and surprise, surprise, here you are sitting in my lounge talking to me."

"We're interviewing you, not interrogating you as a suspect, sir, there's a difference," Sally explained.

"Do us all a favour and get off your high horse, mate," Jack added.

"I'm not on my bleeding high horse. If I was, you'd be the first to recognise it, *mate*," Stanton shot back as soon as Jack had finished.

Sally raised a hand between the two men. "Stop with the testosterone-filled anger, boys, it's not getting us anywhere. As I said, going back to when the murder of Millie Pickrel took place, can you recall anyone hanging around outside the home, *their* home, say a week or so before?"

He scratched the side of his head and then wiped his running nose on the back of his hand. Sally cringed. "Nope, I can't recall, but hey, that was almost twenty years ago. Are you telling me you remember in detail something that happened in your life nearly two decades ago?"

Sally sighed, feeling helpless. He had a point, as much as she hated to admit it. "Okay, that's a fair comment. Please, I'm begging you, try and think back, see if anything out of the ordinary happened which might have caused any likely suspicion around that time?"

Silence filled the room while he thought for a moment or two. Sally's hopes were dashed a few seconds later when he shook his head.

"Nope. I wish I could help, but too much time has elapsed. None of us are getting any younger, are we? Sometimes I can't even frigging remember what I had for dinner the previous day. Sorry."

Sally heaved out a sigh. "It was worth a try. I'll leave you a card, just in case anything comes to mind." She rose from her seat and passed him one of her business cards.

He took it, stood and walked over to the mantelpiece and placed it on top. "I'll put it here for safekeeping."

He then showed them back to the front door.

Sally nodded at him. "Thanks for trying to help us, Mr Stanton."

"Try is the word. I didn't do anything to that child, I swear on my mother's grave, I didn't."

Sally issued the man a weak smile; she believed him. "Ring us if you either think of anything or hear anything over the next few days."

"I will."

They turned up the path and stopped outside their car.

"What now?" Jack asked, eyeing the other properties around them.

"You've guessed it. I know we said we'd pass over the house-to-house to one of the others; however, it seems daft not to throw ourselves into it while we're out here."

He growled. "I hate doing it, you know, when your gut is screaming at you that it's likely going to be a waste of time."

"Let's face it, Jack, you've just described ninety percent of our normal working day."

"That's bloody true enough. Which side do you want to take?"

Sally opened the car door and extracted the file she'd brought with her with all the relevant neighbours' details. "I've got the people we need to speak to noted down here. There are only four still here. That'll make it easier for us, two each."

"If you insist. Ask the same questions we asked of that twerp in there, right?"

"Similar. He has a record, so I admit we went in there heavy-handed. Take it easier on the other neighbours."

"Whatever. And what if this proves to be a waste of time?"

"Ever the optimist, eh, Bullet?"

He shrugged his huge shoulders. "You know me."

"Only too well. Let me know if you hit on anything."

"What, like finding a pot of gold at the end of the rainbow? Not sure that's likely, not after nineteen bloody years."

"Negativity isn't part of my vocabulary, Jack, you should know that by now. Put a smile on your face. That'll transfer to your insides and make the world seem a whole lot brighter, I promise you."

He turned and walked away. "What a crock of poppycock you talk at times," he grumbled.

"I heard that," she called after him.

He peered over his shoulder and grinned. "You were supposed to."

"Get on with it and don't return to the car until you have something worth listening to."

He stopped dead in his tracks. "Are you kidding me?"

"It was worth a shot," she replied, smiling.

He groaned and mumbled something else and then crossed the road.

Sally knocked on the first house on her list. It happened to be two doors down from Stanton's.

An elderly lady with a curved spine opened the door and tilted her head to look at her. "Yes, can I help?"

Sally produced her warrant card. "DI Sally Parker. Are you Mrs Wootton?"

Her hand left the door and clutched the front of her chest. "Oh my, the police! What on earth are the police doing on my doorstep? I haven't done anything wrong. At least, I don't think I have. Oh God, don't tell me my daughter has been in an accident?"

"No, I assure you, it's nothing like that. Please, don't be alarmed, we're here conducting general enquiries. I'm led to believe that you've lived in the same property for nearly thirty years, is that correct?"

"I can't stand for long, dear, would you mind coming in? I need to sit in my special chair in the lounge, and quickly, otherwise my back will play me up for days. It's a damn nuisance, that's what it is. I'll be glad when the good Lord comes to claim me." She strolled back into the house, clearly expecting Sally to follow her.

Sally closed the front door and patiently walked behind the poor woman who appeared to be very unstable on her feet. Sally wondered if she should be living alone if her health had deteriorated so much.

Once the old lady was tucked up in her comfy-looking recliner, she gestured for Sally to sit opposite her in the two-seater, fabric-covered couch on the other side of the gas fire which was on a low heat. "General enquiries, you say. About what, may I ask?"

"A crime that took place almost twenty years ago."

Mrs Wootton shook her head slowly. "I know the one you're talking about. That poor little girl. Buggered if I can remember her name after all this time. Well, she was murdered in her own bed, wasn't she?"

"That's the one. Millie Pickrel."

She snapped her finger and thumb together. "That's it. Poor child." She stared at the floral-patterned carpet beneath her feet and shook her head again. "Poor innocent child."

"Can you remember much about what happened around that time?"

"Nothing wrong with my memory, it's my body that's giving out on me, not my brain. What did you want to know? The family moved away after…well, the child's death."

"I know. I'm in touch with the mother. Something has come to light about the case which has made us reopen it."

"Never? Well, I'll be buggered. After all these years you've finally discovered something to go on. What is it? Can you tell me?"

"Not in that sense, sorry to mislead you. I'm in charge of a cold case team which has been specifically formed to deal with a number of crimes that were investigated by a certain officer. This is one of those crimes."

"Corrupt bastard, was he? I never liked the look of the man. Spoke to me like I was something he'd stepped in, you know, dog's mess."

"Not corrupt, just guilty of neglecting to fulfil his duties correctly."

"That's a polite way of saying he screwed up cases, right?"

"You're very astute, Mrs Wootton. Have you worked for the police?"

"Nope, my brother did, though. Never made it past a constable walking the beat. He used to tell me how difficult it was to rise up the ranks back in the day, intimated that a lot of backhanders went on, if you get my drift."

Sally's stomach clenched into a knot. "So I've heard. It's all changed nowadays, thankfully."

"Let's face it, dear. Something had to change before it declined into being farcical. I recall being none too impressed with this officer's policing skills at the time. When he knocked on my door, it was for a brief chat. I expected him to come back; he never did. Maybe I should have put in a complaint about his work ethic at the time. Trouble with that is, retribution. The police were known for roughing up people who spoke out against them in those days."

"Really? Now that's something I wasn't aware of. I'm sorry you felt you couldn't speak out; however, I totally understand why you didn't. A different world back then, yes?"

"And some. Anyway, I have to ask how the mother is doing."

"She's well. Pleased we've reopened the case. She lives about half an hour away nowadays. She's married with another child, a boy."

"How wonderful. I'm glad she was able to get on with her life after such a tragedy struck her family. And her son?"

"Louie. We've yet to meet him. He's away at present. We're hoping to catch up with him soon."

"Nice boy, he was. Devoted to his little sister. The number of times I saw them walking hand in hand past my window on the way to the shops to pick up something for their mother. Sad day when that precious child left this earth, sad day indeed. Far too young to get the calling, even if she was murdered. I hate that word. It sounds sinister in itself, or is that just me thinking that?"

Sally liked this old lady. She said what she meant and didn't hold back, and it reminded her how her own grandmother used to be when she was alive. Sentimental tears momentarily clouded her vision. "You're right, I've never thought about it that way, but yes, I definitely agree with you. I prefer the word *killed*, although it's the same meaning at the end of the day."

"I suppose so. What is it you want to speak to me about? I'll try and help if I can."

"Going over old ground, hoping to jog someone's memory really. Do you remember much about the incident?"

"Apart from being furious that I felt the investigating officer needed a good shake, you mean?"

"Yes, apart from that. What I'm more interested in is if you can recall any strangers hanging around, perhaps a week or so before the family tragedy struck."

"I thought about it long and hard at the time, thinking that idiot inspector was bound to ask me—he didn't by the way—and no, nothing out of the ordinary struck me as odd. Not that I was ever a sticky beak back then. I was working full time, but the crime took place after I got in from work. I would have noticed a stranger lingering, I assure you. Having a copper in the family makes you extra vigilant."

"I'm sure it does. Is your brother still a copper?"

Her head dropped a little. "No, he died of lung cancer a few years ago. I suppose that's what you get for smoking forty fags a day. He wouldn't be able to afford them these days, what with them being around eight quid a packet or something ridiculous like that."

"Horrible habit. Never seen the fascination with it myself. I'm sorry to hear about your brother. Cancer sucks."

"It does. Our family has been riddled with it over the years. I've managed to dodge it so far. Worse things to deal with, what with this damn spine of mine."

"It looks a painful condition, you have my sympathies."

"Thank you. Nowt the doctors can do, so I sit here all day, waiting for the end to come."

"Oh gosh, don't say that. Have you thought of going into a nursing home? At least you'd have company during the day."

She waved the suggestion away. "Phooey, I'd go downhill rapidly if I was forced to live in one of those damn places. I cope well enough. Can't stand around cooking in the kitchen like I used to do; I tend to rely on a lot of ready meals that I can slam in the microwave and be done with it."

Sally's heart sank for the poor woman. If she had more time on her hands, she would offer to stay with her for an hour and knock up a nutritional meal for her. Saying that, she doubted very much if the woman would have the ingredients lying around in her kitchen, like fresh veg et cetera, by what she'd already said. "They can be nice, so I'm told."

"Hit and miss. I find myself having the same meals every few days because I know they suit my taste. What I wouldn't give for someone to drop by unannounced and whisk me off for a pub lunch. Make my day that would."

"Maybe if you drop a big enough hint to your family, they'll surprise you one day."

"Nope, not going to happen. I'm the last one left. Just me, myself and I."

"Sorry to hear that. Perhaps there's a local club you can go to during the week, something along those lines."

"Not that I've heard of. I'll look into it. The trouble is, I enjoy my own company. Can't stand being false with people. Most of them piss me off really."

Sally chuckled. "I know what you mean."

"Have you had much joy with your investigation?"

"Our investigation is still in its infancy, and no, not so far. Opening up a cold case is so much harder than people realise. We're lucky, insofar as there are five neighbours still living in the area who were around when the crime was committed. You're the second person I've spoken to."

"Who's the other one?"

"Mr Stanton, a few doors down."

"Oh, him. Damn paedo. The likes of him shouldn't be allowed out of prison."

"He's told me it was a mistake. The flip side to that is he's done his time for the crime he committed."

"That's as may be, but…" Mrs Wootton shuddered. "He would be at the top of my list of suspects. Creepy little shit, he is. I refuse to speak to the cretin."

"Has he ever treated you badly?"

"I haven't given him the bloody chance. I keep out of his damn way, always have done."

"Do you get on with the other neighbours?"

"I used to. It was different when we were all working. A cheery hello now and again when we spotted each other either going to or coming home from work. These days, well, frankly, no one seems to give a toss. They much prefer being tucked up in their own safe world behind closed doors."

Sally frowned. "Are you saying that's because of the murder?"

Her head tilted from side to side, and her mouth turned down. "Possibly. Never thought about it until now. Mind, if they felt that way, why on earth wouldn't they move away from the area? Why stick around, reliving what went on back then?"

"No idea, it was just a thought. People get stuck in their ways, resistant to change, I suppose. Anyway, is there anything else you wanted to say to the senior officer in charge back then that you want to say to me?"

"Open to a bit of criticism, are you?"

"I can take it on the chin, I have broad shoulders. Hit me with it," Sally said, smiling.

"You're too nice. I couldn't possibly gun you down. Actually, you've done more today than that waste of space of an inspector did at the time. Prat with a capital P comes to mind. You're thorough, you're asking all the right questions, let's say that."

"I try to. I have a tendency to put myself in other people's shoes and ask the most obvious questions. Not every copper does the same, I'm afraid. I treat people courteously and with respect—again, not every serving police officer can say that."

"You do. My brother was the same. It's a shame he had people standing in his way. He deserved to rise up the ranks, bless him. I miss him, he was a daft bugger, caring sort. We got on well together, a bit like the Pickrel children," she stated, bringing the conversation back to the investigation.

Sally nodded. "I'm sorry he was let down by the force. I wish I could make amends for that. The truth is, I can't."

She waved her hand again. "Not your problem, you have enough on your plate. I fear for you if you're expecting to find some new evidence after all these years. Maybe it would be better to leave well alone, although saying that, I saw the interview on TV with Anna Pickrel. It brought everything flooding back. Her screams that night will live with me until my dying day. I'm surprised she's been able to get on with her life; not sure I could have done the same. We're all different, though, aren't we?"

"We are. I think it took her a few years. Not something she jumped into, getting married and having another child. Her son is seven, I believe." Sally realised she was telling the woman too much information, but there was something about her that was making Sally trust her.

"Each to their own. Wallowing in self-pity never got anyone anywhere, did it?"

"There is that. Okay, it's been lovely chatting with you. I'll leave you a card in case you think of anything when I've gone."

Mrs Wootton took the card, placed it on the coffee table beside her and started to get to her feet.

Sally put a hand on her shoulder and gently pushed her back down. "No, I insist, you sit there. I'll show myself out and make sure the front door is closed behind me."

"If you're sure. I hope you discover something new for the mother's sake. And her son's, of course."

"So do I. Take care of yourself. Think about what I said about finding a local club to attend. It'll do you good to get out of here now and again."

"I'll do that."

Sally left the house and looked across the road to find Jack standing on the doorstep of one of the houses opposite, talking to an elderly gentleman with a bright-red face who appeared to be blocking the way with his determined stance.

Oops! Poor Jack! She moved on to the next witness and spoke briefly to the man at the house, Mr Goran. He remembered the incident but nothing much else around that time. Said he was going through a divorce back then and ended up drunk most nights. He slept through all the flashing lights and was shocked when he was filled in by the other neighbours the following day. Sally had asked the same question she'd asked Mrs Wootton, if he'd possibly seen anyone hanging around who looked suspicious. Mr Goran shrugged and told her he hadn't. Then he wished her luck with the investigation and closed his front door. She crossed the road to join Jack.

She waited at the gate, tapping her foot, until he'd finished speaking with the man. Jack said his farewells and joined her, rolling his eyes as he left the man's garden. They strolled back to the car.

"Waste of bloody time that was," Jack grumbled, reaching for the door handle on his car.

"I know, it was a necessity, though."

"If you say so. Did you get anything out of the resident living in the house you were in for ages?"

"Not really. She was a nice lady. Told me everyone was devastated by the incident, shaken up by it all."

"Yeah, the two I spoke to said pretty much the same thing to me. Not very helpful. They'd hardly be dancing in the streets if news came out a child had been murdered, would they? Like I said before, it's been another waste of time."

"All right, Jack, I can hear how unhappy you are. Let's get back to the station, wind things down for the day, see what tomorrow brings, eh?"

"Let's face it, can't be any worse, or as boring, as it's been today. Ever regret your decision to take on these cold cases?"

Sally knew he'd mention that at some point during the day, he always did. "You're beginning to sound like a broken record, matey. We all knew how tough this was going to be—well, some of us more than others."

"Maybe I need something more challenging to deal with every day. Just saying…"

Sally glanced out of the side window to watch the open countryside pass by, choosing to ignore his final comment. Once Jack was pissed off, there was no talking to him, that much she'd gathered over the years.

They pulled into the station car park around twenty minutes later and trudged up the stairs on weary legs. She walked into the room to find the rest of the team beavering away but wearing the same fed-up expression Jack had plastered on his face.

"I take it your day has been as uneventful as ours then?" Sally asked no one in particular.

Joanna nodded. "We appear to be coming up blank on this one, boss. Every angle we try seems to be a dead end. I've looked through the records around that time, and there were no other intruder/murder cases going on and nothing within a twenty-mile radius since then either. I'm at a loss what to do next."

"Okay, I don't want us getting down about this case. I realise how damn frustrating these investigations can be, this one in particular; however, I think we should persevere with it for at least a week longer. We still have to interview the main witness—Jack and I will be doing that tomorrow. Let's call it a day for now. I'll think things over this evening and come up with a plan in the morning, how's that?"

The team all agreed and shut down their computers for the night. Sally stayed behind after they'd all gone, to tidy her desk. On her way out, she jotted a few things down on the whiteboard. The names of the neighbours and briefly what they'd said, which didn't amount to much. One name on the board drew her eye, that of Louie Pickrel. She closed her eyes and offered up a silent prayer that what he had to tell them would help to open this case up. She left the station not long after.

She rang Simon. "Hi. I'm on my way home. Do you need me to call in to the supermarket for anything?"

"Nope, dinner is all in hand. Hurry home, I miss you."

A smile pushed aside the scowl she'd been wearing for the past few hours. "I've missed you today, too. I'll be fifteen minutes."

"I'll have a glass of wine waiting for you."

"You're a saint."

She ended the call and relaxed into autopilot mode, Simon's

smiling face uppermost in her mind. He was standing on the front step waiting for her when she pulled into the large gravelled drive. This place still managed to take her breath away. His manor house, yes, she still thought of it as *his* home, even after living here for the past year or so.

They shared a kiss, and he hooked an arm around her shoulder as they entered the house side by side through the huge front door.

"It's good to be home. How did the auction go today?"

"Dinner won't be long; your wine is waiting for you in the kitchen."

She shrugged off his arm and eyed him warily. "What's going on? I know you well enough by now to know when something is afoot, Simon Bracknall."

"You'll see for yourself in a moment. I need to check on the dinner."

She followed him into the vast kitchen and sat at the large oak table. They had their own regular spots, and sitting next to her glass of wine was a sheet of paper. "What's this? Wow, don't tell me you and Dad have bought this today?" She held the paper in her hand and stared at the stunning Georgian mansion. Flipping over the page, she saw that it had ten acres of land and a long, tree-lined drive leading up to the house. The place was simply stunning.

"Nope, nothing to do with the business. You like?"

She stared at him, her mouth gaping open for a second. "I'd have to be nuts to say no."

"Good. It's our new home."

Her mouth dropped open again. She blinked half a dozen times as tears filled her eyes. He came towards her, his glass of wine in his hand, and gestured for her to raise her own glass.

He clinked hers and repeated, "You like?"

Sally gulped down half of her wine. "Are you kidding me? It's absolutely beautiful. What's not to like?"

He sank into the chair next to her and exhaled a large breath. "Bloody hell, that's a relief. I thought you'd be livid with me for choosing our new home without you."

"No way, buster. You have far more knowledge about these things, and better taste, I hasten to add. Why on earth would I be upset with you? You're such a numpty at times."

"Sorry, all this is new, you know, the relationship side of things. I've been pacing the kitchen for the past few hours, wondering if I'd done the right thing or not. The opportunity presented itself, and it was just too good to turn down."

"Does Dad know? He was there with you, yes?"

"No, he doesn't know. We bought a large house that we're going to renovate into four flats. He was dealing with the paperwork on that one when this baby came up. I took a punt that you'd like it and, well, once I'd noted my interest in the property, I got carried away. Before I knew what had happened, the auctioneer was banging his gavel."

"Oh shit, that sounds ominous. Dare I ask how much you paid for it?"

"It was a snip at nine hundred and fifty grand. Six bedrooms, four bathrooms, and an indoor swimming pool and gym. No excuse for either of us to put on weight with those as a constant reminder, eh?"

"Oh my, seriously? You spent just shy of a million on a new home for us?"

"We can afford it, don't start panicking."

"I'm not. Crap, what about this place? You love this house, Simon."

"I know. But it's time to move on. Have I done the wrong thing?"

She reached for his hand. "No, you haven't done the wrong thing, it's just your generosity has floored me. As long as I spend the rest of my life with you, I'd happily live in a two-up, two-down."

He tilted his head and raised his eyebrows. "Who are you trying to kid, Sally Bracknall?"

Her new name still sounded funny even to her own ears. "All right, maybe I slightly misquoted myself there. You didn't have to do this, though, Simon. We both love this place, we'd have been just as happy living here."

He shook his head and laughed.

"Hey, what's so funny?" she asked, frowning.

He tapped the house details with his forefinger. "You haven't even looked at the address, have you?"

She picked up the sheet of paper, looked at it, and then stared at him, dumbstruck.

He nodded. "It's right next door to Lorne and Tony's new place."

"Oh my God, what did I ever do to deserve a man like you? You're one in a bloody million, you truly are, Simon." She leaned forward to kiss him.

They shared a lingering kiss until Simon broke away and leapt out of his chair.

"Damn, the fish will be burnt soon. Are you ready for dinner?"

"I'll lay the table. I'm so excited, I doubt I'll be able to eat much, despite being hungry on the way home. I can't wait to break the news to Lorne."

He dished up the broccoli and beans, the chickpea mash, which was a speciality of his, and the salmon steaks which he'd coated in red pesto. It was one of her favourite meals. "Let's not say anything until we go over there at the weekend."

There was a twinkle in his eye.

She nodded. "You're a devious man."

"When I have to be. I'm so glad you're happy about this, Sal."

"If you were worried I'd be upset, then you really don't know me at all, do you?"

"I have a lot to learn, I know." They sat at the table with their meals, and he raised his glass. "To us and our future neighbours."

"To us, and to you, for being the most generous, kind-hearted, adorable man I have ever met."

His cheeks flushed. "To you, for making me the happiest man alive when you became my wife."

"Hark at us, soppy bloody pair. If ever two people belonged together, it's us, right?"

"I agree wholeheartedly. Now eat your dinner. I hope it's not too spoilt."

"It's fine. Looks and smells delicious."

The meal went down a treat after her stressful and frustrating day.

Simon insisted on loading the dishwasher and encouraged her to put her feet up in the lounge while he made a pot of fresh coffee.

Sally was going over the details of the property for the tenth time when he joined her. Her heart was still bursting with joy. "I love it. What a spectacular place. Can we go and see it soon?"

"Maybe I can arrange a visit at the weekend, kill two birds and all that."

"Brilliant, yes, let's do that. I've just realised something…"

"What's that?"

"You've just bought the place without even stepping inside it. That's insane."

He laughed and tipped back his head. "Welcome to my world. It's what your father and I do all the time."

She punched him on the arm. "That's different, and you know it. This is our home I'm talking about here."

He pulled a face. "You have a point. What if the photos are fake?"

She sat upright in her chair and felt the colour drain from her face. "No, don't say that. They wouldn't do that." He laughed again, and she swiped his arm. "Shit, you nearly gave me a heart attack then."

"Just testing, to see if you were on your toes."

"I can do without tests like that. What on earth are we going to do with six bedrooms? Think of all the furniture we're going to have to buy to fill the damn place. And the council tax is going to be horrendous on a house that size."

He tutted and shook his head. "Stop worrying. It's all in hand, never fear. Where property is concerned, Sally Bracknall, I'm an expert."

She snuggled into him. "I'm glad you are. I'm shite at making a home feel like a home. Hey, I bet Lorne will have some advice to share with us. She used to renovate houses herself once upon a time."

"I'm open to suggestions, although I think she'll have enough on her hands to deal with running the kennels and decorating her new place."

"There is that. She's going to be bloody thrilled when we tell her."

5

Sally ended up being far too excited to sleep. She crept downstairs around one and, with her notebook in hand, settled down on the couch with a quilt, making notes on where next to go with the investigation. She and Simon had briefly discussed the case before going to bed. Maybe that was why she found it impossible to sleep. He was going to search the files from the post-mortem and see if there was anything he could find to help them.

She finally dropped off around three.

Simon woke her at seven with a mug of coffee and a welcome kiss. "There you go, princess. You eventually managed to grab some sleep then."

She sat up. "I did. My head was spinning. I've never known a case get to me as much as this one."

"Really? I think you've mentioned that before on other cases."

She smiled. "Oops, sorry to be so repetitive."

"Do you think it has something to do with a child being involved?"

"I don't think so. Who knows?" She placed her mug on the table beside her and threw back the quilt. "I'd better get a wriggle on. I've made a decision that I don't think will go down well with some members of the team."

Goodbye My Precious child

"Are you going to tell me what that is?" he called out after her as she flew upstairs and into the bathroom.

Fifteen minutes later, she was dressed and ready to go. Still full from the previous evening's dinner, she decided to skip breakfast, much to Simon's displeasure.

When she entered the station, she found Jack and Joanna both hard at work. "I'll be in my office. Let me know when the others arrive. I have something important to tell you all."

She spotted the puzzled look that drifted between Jack and Joanna.

Jack turned to face her. "Are you teasing us again?"

She grinned. "Not in the slightest." Sally slipped into her office to tackle the post. Thankfully, there wasn't much to deal with today, so she took out her notebook and flipped through the notes she'd made during the night.

Jack poked his head into the room a few minutes later. "All present and awaiting further instruction, boss."

She smiled at him and nodded. "I'll be right there. I could do with a coffee."

"I'll sort that out for you if you give me a hint as to what you're about to say."

Sally laughed. "You're a trier, I'll give you that, Jack."

He left, and she followed him out a few minutes later. She walked across the room to the stack of files they were yet to go through and plucked one off the top. "Okay, here's the deal. I sensed everyone was super frustrated yesterday, I was as well. Therefore, I think we should split the team up."

"Meaning what exactly?" Jack asked, crossing one leg over the other at the knee.

"Jack and I, maybe Joanna as well, will remain on the Pickrel case, while Jordan and Stuart begin delving into this one. Joanna can work on both cases if needed. Everyone agree with that?"

Joanna was the first to speak up. "I'm fine with it. The busier I am the better at the end of the day. Can't stand sitting around twiddling my damn thumbs, you know that, boss."

"I do. What about you, gents?" she asked Jordan and Stuart.

"Aye, suits me," Stuart replied.

"And me," Jordan agreed.

Sally stepped forward with the file and handed it to Stuart. "I'll leave that with you then. Any problems, get back to me, and we'll go over it together."

"Will do, boss," Stuart said.

"Let's get you guys started. The case is the murder of a woman who was allegedly poisoned by her husband, Lucinda Barratt. This took place in twenty-sixteen. Mick Barratt has been in prison since then and has always profusely protested his innocence. Let's get to the bottom of that."

"You want us to visit Barratt in prison?" Stuart asked.

It'll save me having to go out there again so soon. "Yes, that would be a good starting point. Primarily, get a feel for his demeanour. In my experience, you can usually tell if someone sitting in jail is guilty or not. Go from there. If you think along the lines that he's innocent, then ask who he thinks poisoned his wife and why. What possible motive could they have? Had anyone fallen out with either of them before the incident happened? You get my drift, dig deep. Grab the opportunity to grill him, if he's up to it. But first, have a word with the staff to see what his state of mind is. If he's fragile, then take it easy on him. Oh God, you know all this, I'm teaching you how to suck eggs. Call me a control freak." She grinned. "Ring the prison to get the all clear, then spend the next thirty minutes getting acquainted with the case. Any doubts, you know where I am."

Both men nodded, and Jordan moved his chair closer to Stuart's desk and got stuck in.

"What about us? What are we going to do?" Jack asked unenthusiastically.

"You know what lies ahead of us today, partner. We'll be heading out to see the man himself, Louie Pickrel. He asked us to be at his house at ten."

"Whoopie doo!" Jack replied.

Sally shook her head and returned to her office. She knew there was little point talking to her partner when he was in one of his sarcastic moods. *Let's hope the coffee changes his way of thinking before we leave.*

Fordacre Road was in a quiet area. The road contained six houses with even fewer cars on the drives. A gentleman was tending his roses in the front garden of the first house and looked up when they drove past.

"Seems a reasonable area," Jack commented after hardly speaking during the trip.

"Quiet and subdued with an inquisitive neighbour by the look of things."

"You mean nosy," he corrected her.

"That too." She heaved out a breath and switched off the engine. "Let's get this over with. Can't say I'm looking forward to meeting him. Daft thing to say, but I think it's going to be an emotional affair."

"For you maybe."

"You've got a heart of stone at times, Jack Blackman."

"Whatever."

She shook her head, and they both left the vehicle. Sally took in her surroundings. It didn't take her long to realise that the Pickrels' house was immaculate compared to some of the others. Possibly freshly painted. The front garden on both sides of the block paving path had a neatly trimmed lawn with an abundance of flowering shrubs in the borders. In the air was the smell of newly cut grass. Had someone been out there already that morning?

Jack rang the bell. The door opened within a few moments. A man in his early thirties welcomed them with a broad smile.

Sally produced her ID. "Mr Pickrel? I'm DI Sally Parker, and this is Jack Blackman, my partner."

"We've been expecting you. Please come in. Would you like a drink?"

Sally smiled and nodded. "A coffee would be lovely," she replied, stepping over the threshold.

Jack followed her and closed the door behind him.

Pickrel led them through to the back of the house into a kitchen which was adjoined by a vast orangery that took Sally's breath away.

He seemed pleased by her amazed expression. "A new addition we put on a year ago."

"It's beautiful."

"Thank you. This is my wife, Natalie." He placed an arm around her shoulder and patted her distended stomach with his other hand. "And baby makes three."

He and his wife chuckled, as if they'd shared a private joke.

Sally extended her hand to the petite brunette. "Pleased to meet you. How long to go?"

"Two months. Longest seven months of my life so far," she said, her tone full of exhaustion.

"Oh dear, has it been a bad pregnancy?" Sally asked.

"Understatement of the decade, eh, Louie?"

He pecked her lovingly on the nose. "Don't go into detail, love. I'm sure the officers don't want to hear about all our woes."

"It's fine," Sally replied. "Let's hope the final two months are easier for you."

"Thank you. I'll make a drink. Tea or coffee?" Natalie asked, unhooking herself from her husband's attentive grip.

Sally smiled. "We've already put an order in with your husband. Two coffees, milk and sugar, thanks."

"Two sugars for me," Jack said.

Natalie left them and headed towards the kitchen area.

"Please, take a seat," Louie instructed, motioning for them to sit at the large rectangle oak table with its comfy padded chairs.

Natalie joined them a few moments later. Louie was the one who handed the mugs around after Natalie told him who they belonged to.

Sally took a sip of coffee, either preparing herself or delaying her first question, she wasn't sure which.

"Have you had any joy with the investigation?" Louie asked, placing his hands around his mug.

"Not so far, no. It's still early days. Thank you for taking the time to see us. Hopefully, we'll be able to make more of an impact into the case once we've listened to your side of the events. I know how difficult this is going to be for you. Just take your time; stop to have a breather if you feel the need to."

He nodded and looked at his wife, smiled at her, and then glanced down at his mug again. "Okay, forgive me if it all gets too much, it's still very raw for me, even after all these years. She was the sweetest child ever, and I miss her terribly." His voice caught in his throat.

"Take your time. We've got all day if necessary."

"Thank you. We'd been out that day, a day out in Great Yarmouth. We didn't have too many of those I seem to remember as a kid. Money was excruciatingly tight when we were little. Mum did her best, but with no father around, life was tougher for us than my friends at school. The thing that kept us going was our love for each other." He shook his head. "I still have nightmares about that night."

"He does. I can vouch for that. Wakes up in a cold sweat at least once a month, maybe more," Natalie threw in.

"I'm sorry to hear that, Louie, and yet they say time is the greatest healer," Sally replied, gulping down the emotion rising within her, then taking a swig of her coffee to help keep it at bay. Her own life flashed before her eyes for a second or two. Yes, she herself had healed, now that she was married to Simon. All that went on during her marriage to Darryl was in her distant past. She hoped Louie would feel the same way in the future, perhaps when the baby was born.

"Life deals us a wrong card now and again, Inspector. I don't think I'll ever get over what happened that night, especially as we'd had the perfect family day out."

"If it's not too difficult for you, maybe you could go over the details for us?"

"I'll do my best. You'll have to forgive me if I break down. My sister meant the world to me," he repeated.

"No problem. I completely understand."

He sipped his drink then started again. "We spent the day at the large pool at Great Yarmouth. Mum watched on from the lounger; she was busy reading one of her books; it was one of the classics, can't remember which one, not that it matters. Anyway, she wasn't really one for splashing around in the water. Millie and I didn't mind, we had fun all the same. We spent most of the time going down the slide—that was my sister's favourite part." He paused, no doubt as his sister's fun-loving nature filled his mind. "She was never happier than when she was with me. I cared for her deeply, protected her, not that she needed protecting much on a day-to-day basis. I could do little to protect her that night, though. Yes, I chased after the man, but…well, the damage had already been done."

"I'm so sorry you had to witness that as a child. What age were you?"

"Twelve. Only twelve and to be confronted with that at such a young age, well, I haven't really been able to put into words over the years how I felt exactly. Unless you're ever in that position yourself, I don't think you'll ever know." He wiped a hand over his brow that had broken out in a sweat.

Sally's stomach constricted. She hated putting this man through this horrendous ordeal again after all these years. He was obviously still distraught by what had gone on that night. Who wouldn't be? "There's no rush," she reminded him.

He tilted his head back and let out an agonisingly long breath.

Natalie reached for his hand. "It's all right, darling, take a breather. In your own time."

He smiled and leaned over to kiss her on the cheek. "I'm glad you're with me. Not sure I could go through this again on my own."

"Have you sought help from counsellors over the years?" Sally asked.

"Several of them have tried to help me but failed. I got the impression they thought I was screwed up, you know, in my head. I suppose they're right."

"Anyone in your shoes would probably be feeling the same as you. Try not to be too hard on yourself, Louie."

"That's what I keep telling him," Natalie said, stroking her hand along his forearm.

"It's hard not to. To be that close to that man…as he sucked the life out of her. Oh God, why? Why did he have to do that? She was loved. Protected. Cared for like no other child I knew, and where did it get her in the end? Death, it's so final. Death, it haunts all my days and nights. I've tried so many times over the years to come to terms with my grief. But hell, to be that close and yet I could do nothing to save her… I tried to revive Millie. Tried to breathe life back into her lifeless body. I failed. I'm such a failure."

"You're not a *failure*, Louie. No one would ever regard you as that," Natalie tried to reassure him.

"Your wife is right, Louie. You need to get past this. It's been almost twenty years, and you have your whole life ahead of you. A baby of your own to look forward to," Sally pointed out.

"I know. I'm grateful to Natalie for taking me on. She's a very special lady." He smiled at his wife, and her cheeks flushed.

"And you have a beautiful home in which to welcome your son or daughter."

He nodded. "I hope it's a girl—no, I'm praying it's a girl." He gathered his wife's hands in his and smiled lovingly at her. "We're going to call her Millie, aren't we, love?"

Sally nodded. Anna had told her that, and it still struck a bum note with her.

"Your mother mentioned that when we saw her. Isn't that a bit strange?" Jack asked, apparently tapping into Sally's thoughts.

Sally watched the couple's reaction to the question.

Louie slowly turned to face Jack. "She's fine with it. She's looking forward to having her first grandchild. Anyway, we don't know if it's going to be a boy or a girl yet. We'll cross that bridge in a couple of months. I'm sure whatever we decide to name it, Mum will back us, she always does. She's an excellent mother who has always put her children first, except for that night."

Sally couldn't tell if she'd detected some bitterness in his tone.

"Your mother was out on a date with a man at the time, is that correct?"

"Yes. She got a child to look after us. That child left us alone the minute she got a phone call from home."

"Lisa's father also died that evening, didn't he?" Sally pressed gently.

"Yes. It was a tragic set of circumstances that evening which culminated in two deaths."

"Am I right in thinking that you blame your mother for leaving you with the babysitter then?"

He threw a hand up in the air. "I don't know. I've tried to make sense of the situation in my head over the years, and none of it makes sense at all. If Mum hadn't gone out on a date, would any of it have happened? Millie's death and the death of Lisa's father? Who knows?"

"Has your mother blamed herself over the years?"

He shook his head. "Not to that extent. She came to terms with Millie's death quickly and moved on. Married that man, and they had another son soon after."

Anna had seemed pretty emotional about her daughter's death. Was she acting? "What would be the point in your mother dwelling on the past? Over something that she couldn't change, no matter how hard she tried? Wasn't it her first date in a while?"

"Yes. Does that make a difference?" he bit back swiftly.

"Not in the slightest, I was merely stating a fact. Mr Pickrel, is there something you're not telling us about that night?"

He looked her in the eye, his gaze narrowing for a split second before returning to normal. "Such as?"

"As your mother wasn't at the premises, could she have arranged for this to have happened?" Sally had no idea where that question had come from. She felt three sets of eyes turn her way and wriggled in her seat uncomfortably. "I'm sorry, I shouldn't have asked such a damning question."

Louie nodded. "No, you shouldn't have. How can you possibly think my mother is behind this? Are you insane? She gave up her whole life to care and provide for us kids. It was her first date since she left that no-good father of mine. She had the right to go out and enjoy herself that evening. She'd done everything she could to ensure we'd had a good time at the pool during the day. Why shouldn't she go out on a date?" His voice rose along with his anger.

Natalie gathered his hand in hers. He pulled it away and sat back, clearly offended.

Sally felt awful. "I didn't mean to cause offence. I'm sorry."

"You're no better than him," Louie replied, venom rife in his tone.

"Him? Who, the killer?" Sally demanded, offended herself to be compared to a man who could take a child's life.

"Not the killer, that waste of space detective who came to our house."

Sally shook her head. "I'm sorry you think that way. I truly didn't mean anything by my question. Please, forget I mentioned it."

"That's hard to do." He prodded the side of his temple. "It's already embedded up here, just like the rest of it."

Sally ran a hand across her face. "Sometimes I speak before I engage my brain; that's clearly what's happened on this occasion. I can't apologise enough. Perhaps you can tell me how you think the intruder got in that night?"

He remained silent for a few moments. Sally sensed he was trying to get hold of his temper. She couldn't blame him. She hated herself at that moment.

Eventually, he said, "I went to the toilet and when I came back the man was in the bedroom. His hands forcing the pillow over my sister's face. She wasn't moving; I knew she was gone. I shouted at him, asked him what he was up to. He gasped, hadn't expected to see me there, I suppose. I chased him and he couldn't get out of the window quick enough, I locked it in case he thought about returning, then I rang nine-nine-nine, and they helped me to perform the CPR procedure. It was difficult trying to revive her, knowing that she was already dead and I was the one tasked with trying to make her heart start again." He paused.

Natalie ran her hand along his forearm again.

He smiled at her and placed a loving hand on her cheek. "Thank you, love. You've heard this story so many times since we met. I'm grateful to have you in my life and by my side."

"I wouldn't be anywhere else. I love you, Louie, you're a very special man. A woman couldn't ask for a more loving husband. Hopefully, when the baby comes, it will help alleviate some of your problems."

"I hope so, too," he replied.

Sally watched the touching scene with a lump bulging in her throat. She coughed to try to shift it. She decided to take her time in asking any further questions, thinking it would be insensitive for her to intrude.

"What else do you need to know, Inspector?" Louie finally asked, holding his wife's hand tightly.

"How difficult was it for you to remember the man's features at the time, on top of everything else?"

"So-so. I said I wanted to work with a sketch artist quickly before I forgot. Although, I have to say, my memory is exceptional."

"I can vouch for that. My husband has never missed a birthday or anniversary yet," Natalie interjected with a broad grin.

"I've always been the type to put others first. Their needs are greater than mine. That's why I loved playing with my sister, spending time with her."

"I understand. What was the inspector's reaction to the E-FIT you created?"

He shrugged. "Nonplussed, I suppose. He said that he would circulate it amongst his men. To my knowledge, it was never mentioned again."

"You didn't see it featured on the news or in the newspapers?" Sally asked.

"Mum kept me sheltered from those, said I'd gone through enough tackling the intruder as it was."

Sally nodded, understanding Anna's dilemma. Louie had been a mere child himself at the time and had suffered enough that day. "Going back to the intruder, did he say anything to you? Or did you say anything to him?"

"I gasped when I saw him. He turned and hesitated for a moment or two, then bolted. I think he was in two minds whether to hang around and kill me as well. That's the impression I got anyway. All I could think of was to get him out of the house, to help save Millie. Maybe if I had reacted quicker…"

"Don't think like that, love, you did your best," Natalie said, picking up his hand and kissing it as if it were a treasured little kitten or puppy.

"Natalie is right, Louie, there's no point blaming yourself. You were a child. Children tend to react differently to adults in these situations."

His eyes watered. "Even so. I should've tried harder, sooner. That regret will always live with me. A so-near-and-yet-so-far kind of moment we all experience at some point in our lives."

"I get that," Sally concurred. "It's not helping you to get over the trauma, however, and it's time for you to do that now that you have a child of your own on the way."

"I'm hoping that will be the key to my future." He glanced up at Sally and then faced Natalie and said, "Our future together."

"Okay, I think we have enough to go on now. If you're sure there's nothing else you can recall?"

"I'm sorry, I wish there was."

Sally finished the remains of her coffee and stood. Jack flipped his notebook shut and rose from his seat, too. Natalie was the one who offered to show them out. Louie's head sank, and he stayed seated at the table.

"Thank you for seeing us today. I know it must've been hard for you to relive what went on. I appreciate you putting yourself through such torment for our benefits. You have my word that we'll do our very best to deliver the justice you and your mother have been seeking all these years. I apologise the original investigation didn't run as smoothly as it should have under Inspector Falkirk's guidance."

He stared at his hands and said, "All we ask is that you do your best, Inspector. We look forward to hearing from you in the near future."

They left the room, and Natalie held the front door open for them.

"We're sorry you had to hear all that. I truly didn't want you to get upset, what with your due date being so close. Thank you for listening to Louie's side of events and comforting him when he needed it."

"You're welcome. He doesn't talk about it much, but I often see him drifting off and I'm sure he's constantly reliving that dreadful time in his life. Putting myself in his shoes, I doubt I would have coped as well."

"It takes a special person to be able to carry on after being involved in something so traumatic. I'm glad he has you by his side should he ever decide to open up and reveal his true feelings," Sally replied.

"I'll be here for however long it takes. I think the baby will change a lot when he or she finally enters this world."

"Take it easy until they make an appearance. Thanks, Natalie. We'll be in touch if we have any news for you."

Natalie closed the door gently behind them. As she walked down the path, Sally looked over her shoulder at the house.

"What's up?" Jack asked.

"I don't know, I got the impression that the house is full of anguish. I hope that alters now that he's spoken with us, for the baby's sake."

"A terrible situation to find themselves in. I dread to think how I'd feel if anything happened to either of my two, or my granddaughter come to that. It'd likely destroy me."

Sally patted him on the back. "You're a good man, Jack, deep down."

"Hmm…meaning what? That I'm generally a bastard?"

Sally chuckled. "There you go again, twisting my damn words. You said the B word, not me."

They were back at the car by now.

"Open the damn door," he grumbled.

She swallowed down the laugh that was desperate to escape and slipped behind the steering wheel.

Attaching his seat belt, he asked, "What now? It's not as if he told us something we didn't already know."

"That's true enough. Back to the station and put our heads together, I suppose. I'm going to ring Simon. He mentioned last night that he was going to check the PM report for me, see if anything shows up there. Apart from that, I'd say we're screwed. We've questioned everyone we can think of who was connected to the case and come up with a big fat zero."

Jack was silent for a few moments. Sally placed the car into first and drove back to the station.

"There's one person we haven't spoken to yet," Jack said, a few minutes into the journey.

"Who?" Sally asked, her forehead furrowing.

"The guy the mother went on a date with that night."

Sally chewed on her bottom lip and then nodded slowly. "You're right. Let's see if we can track him down and rectify that."

"Want me to ring Joanna? It'll save us trawling all the way back to the station."

"Good thinking."

Jack used his own mobile to contact the station. Joanna managed to locate Dean Sutton's address, virtually straight away.

"Get a place of work as well, Jack, just in case."

Joanna heard without Jack having to repeat the request.

"Brilliant, thanks, Joanna. We'll head over there now and then back to base. Everything all right at that end?" Jack said.

"Put it on speaker, Jack," Sally instructed.

"Everything's fine here. Stuart and Jordan are on their way to the prison to interview Mick Barratt, so I'm here alone and enjoying the peace and quiet."

"Good. We shouldn't be too long, Joanna, we wouldn't want you getting used to the solitude," Sally replied, laughing.

"No fear of that, boss. Ugh…I can't find where he's working on either of the systems, sorry."

"Don't be, it was a long shot. We'll drop by the house, see if anyone is at home. If not, we'll see what the neighbours can tell us."

"Okay, good luck."

Jack ended the call. The address Joanna had given them turned out to be ten minutes up the road. They pulled up outside the executive home, and Jack let out a whistle.

"Bloody hell. There's some wealth around here, looking at these pads."

"You're not wrong. I'm trying to think back to what Anna said about his job. He was a colleague of hers, I remember that much."

Jack shrugged. "Can't recall, sorry. I'm guessing he's done pretty darn well for himself."

"Let's take a punt, see if he's in." Sally exited the car and joined Jack on the wide path that led through the beautifully manicured front garden which had box-hedge knot gardens on either side. Sally rang the bell. No answer, so she rang it again. It was promptly opened by a young woman in her early thirties, wearing a grey pin-striped suit.

"Yes, can I help you?"

Sally held up her ID. "DI Sally Parker and DS Jack Blackman. And you are?"

"Katherine Sutton. What's this about?" she demanded abruptly.

"Nothing to be worried about, Mrs Sutton. We're actually after your husband."

"Dean? Why? What's he supposed to have done?" She folded her arms and scowled.

"Nothing. We're conducting general enquiries into a previous investigation."

"You are? As far as I know, my husband has never been involved in any investigation. You'll have to enlighten me."

"We'd much prefer to speak to your husband in person. He can relay the information to you if he wishes."

"Good luck in finding him then." She started to close the door in their faces, but Jack was quick to react and stuck his foot in the gap. "Get away from my house. I know my rights. You need a warrant to come in this house."

"Please, Mrs Sutton, all we're requesting is the address of where your husband works so that we can visit him, today preferably."

"I won't tell you that until you've told me what your visit is regarding."

Sally blew out an exasperated breath. "Very well. It's to do with an investigation that took place nearly twenty years ago."

"For Christ's sake, why didn't you just come out and say that? Why did you have to go out of your way to get me worked up?"

"I wasn't aware that I said anything to warrant you getting uptight, Mrs Sutton. Now, if you'd just tell me where your husband works, we'll let you get on with your day."

"I'll get you one of his business cards." She left the door open and went back in the house, returning a few moments later to hand Sally a card.

Sally read the address and nodded. "We know where that is. Thank you for your help, Mrs Sutton."

"You're welcome." She shut the front door again.

"Bloody rude cow," Jack grumbled on the way back to the car.

"I suppose it was a shock to find two coppers standing on her doorstep. She was dressed in a business suit. Perhaps she was on one of those conference calls. Maybe she works from home and we disturbed her."

"Whatever, there was no need for her to be rude."

Sally sniggered. "You are funny when you're angry. A little tic goes off near your right eye, did you know that?"

"Bollocks, it does not."

A few minutes later they arrived at the industrial estate, situated out in the middle of the countryside. Sutton Systems was the first unit they saw as they entered the site. They walked into the reception area and a slim blonde, with spectacles perched on the end of her nose came towards them.

"Hello, can I help you?"

Sally and Jack produced their IDs. "Is Mr Sutton available for a quick chat?"

"Oh, yes, I believe he's free right now. Just a second, I'll check if he'll see you." She tottered on five-inch heels to the back of the reception area and disappeared out of sight. She returned with a suited man in his early fifties.

He strode past the receptionist and approached them. "I'm Dean Sutton. What can I do for you?"

"We'd like a quiet chat, Mr Sutton," Sally said, looking over at the receptionist and then back at Sutton.

"You'd better come through. Would you like a drink?" He opened the hatch in the reception counter, allowing them access.

"A coffee would be nice, thank you," Sally replied, speaking for both of them.

"Candice, can you sort two coffees out for me? Make it three, I have a feeling I'm going to need one. Come into my office. You'll have to excuse the mess, I'm in the process of searching for a lost invoice."

He stepped into the office and motioned for them to take a seat in front of his desk. There was no floor space to be seen as it was littered with paperwork.

"Oh dear, you certainly have a daunting task on your hands, Mr Sutton."

"Yep, beginning to regret volunteering to find the invoice myself. Thought I'd have it done and dusted within thirty minutes. This is the result, four hours later."

"I don't envy you. Nine times out of ten that type of thing is under your nose."

"I was due to take a breather. I'll go over things again once our meeting is over. May I ask why you're here?"

Candice walked into the office with a tray of mugs and placed it on the edge of his desk. "I wasn't sure if you wanted milk and sugar."

"Thanks, Candice, we'll sort it from here. Shut the door on your way out, please."

Once the door had shut and Dean had distributed the mugs, he sat back and asked, "Have I done something wrong? Sorry, I didn't catch your names."

"I'm DI Sally Parker, and my partner is DS Jack Blackman. No, I want to reassure you from the outset that this is a general enquiry, sir, nothing to be concerned about."

"Good, I don't like surprises. I'm listening, Inspector."

"The reason we're here is because we run a cold case team and we've recently begun investigating a crime that was committed nineteen years ago."

He sat upright in his chair.

"I see that rings a bell with you."

"It does. You're talking about the Millie Pickrel case, aren't you?"

"I am."

He shook his head slowly. "Such a shock. You're aware her mother and I were out on a date that evening? Of course you are, you wouldn't be here otherwise," he said, answering his own question swiftly. He ran a hand through his short black hair that was obviously dyed, judging by his grey eyebrows.

"It was a shocking incident. Perhaps you can tell us what happened?"

He took a sip of his coffee and let out a large sigh. "It's something that will remain with me until the day I die. No one, man, woman or child should ever have to deal with such circumstances."

"I agree."

"Let me think. I turned up at the flat about six-fifty that evening. I spoke to the kids in the living room while Anna finished getting ready. She looked stunning as I recall, a sequinned top over a pair of trousers. The kids seemed happy their mum was going out, and they appeared to take to me in such a short space of time. Anyway, I drove to an Italian restaurant I knew around twenty minutes from where she lived; I still use the same restaurant today."

"Okay, carry on."

"We were halfway through the main course when Anna received a call from the babysitter—sorry, her name escapes me at present."

"Lisa."

He nodded. "That's it. She was frantic, and rightly so. Her father had suffered a suspected heart attack. As soon as I realised something was wrong, I gestured for the waiter to bring us the bill. Poor Anna was beside herself. She told Lisa to leave the kids—we were only twenty minutes away, for God's sake. She also instructed Lisa to close the door when she left. I'll admit I broke the speed limit to get back to those kids. I'll never forget what happened when we arrived." He took a sip of coffee then continued. "The street was lit up with flashing blue lights. There was an ambulance outside the flat. At first, Anna looked at me in confusion, and then we both ran inside. We found two paramedics at the scene trying to resuscitate little Millie. We found Louie standing at the bottom of the bed. The poor lad was in a traumatised state. Not long after, the paramedic working on Millie stood back and shook his head. Anna screamed, I'll never forget that. She dropped to the floor. I tried to comfort her, but she shouted at me to leave the house. I didn't want to intrude on her grief, and as much as I wanted to stay there to support her and Louie, I respected her wishes and left."

"I see. Did you see anyone lingering outside the flat?"

"No. I didn't look. I had no idea what had happened. That didn't come out until the media got hold of the story a few days later."

"Did you try to contact Anna?"

"Yes, of course I did; she didn't want to know. Eventually, Louie took my call and told me in no uncertain terms not to contact his mother ever again. To leave her alone. I had to accept that. The last thing I wanted to do was make their lives more unpleasant than they already were. That child was such a sweetheart. I only met her for a fleeting moment, but she was an absolute doll. Why would anyone in their right minds set out to kill her? The press said it was an intruder, is that right?"

Sally shrugged. "After speaking to all the neighbours and witnesses, we have come to that conclusion. Nothing else has surfaced at this time."

"Is that it? After all these years, that poor family are no further forward?"

"Regarding the case, yes. We still have avenues we want to explore, but it's not looking hopeful so far. Have you seen Anna since that day?"

"No. She left her job, never returned after the…Millie died. I was tempted to go round there, but Louie was adamant that would be a bad idea. So I left well alone. Have you seen her? Stupid question, of course you have. Is she well?"

"She's well. Still riddled with guilt, but she's married with another child."

"I'm so glad. It's wrong to live in the past. Grief is a powerful emotion, I know. I lost my father only last month; I'm still not over his death. Some people bounce back, and for others the grieving process can be a long, drawn-out affair. I have to admit, I have to focus heavily when I'm here. My wife insisted it would be better for me to get back to work as soon as possible." He smiled. "She works from home, you see, didn't want me getting under her feet, truth be told."

"I got that impression. Are you sure there's nothing else you can tell us?"

He pondered for a little while and then shook his head. "No. I'm sorry. Over the years, I suppose I've programmed myself to block out that evening. Part of me recognises that's the wrong decision, but the other part thinks I was within my rights not to dwell on the incident. I couldn't change anything. Anna and I were out on an innocent date. I regret taking her away from her children; however, she could have always declined my invitation. She didn't. The result was devastating to all of us in the end."

"These things happen in life. If everyone possessed a crystal ball or a time machine, well, we'd all be far wiser than we are. Thanks for seeing us today, Mr Sutton. Sorry if it brought it all back to you."

"No need to apologise. Do you think you'll catch the bastard? I mean, after all these years, is that even likely?"

Sally shrugged and left her seat. "We can but try. We appreciate you seeing us at such short notice anyway."

He walked with them back out into the reception area and shook their hands. "My door is always open if you need to run anything past me."

"That's good to know, thank you. Good day, sir."

"Another false avenue that led us nowhere," Jack muttered as they strode back to the car.

"Yep. We're not getting very far on this one at all. Come on, I'll buy us all a cream cake to cheer us up."

They stopped off at the baker's close to the station, and Sally bought three cream slices, knowing that two of her team would be out of the office when they got back.

Over coffee and cake, she, Jack and Joanna went over and over the details pertaining to the case so far and drew a blank whichever way they looked at the evidence in their possession so far.

"Where do we turn to next?" Jack asked, leaning back in his chair and placing his hands on his head.

"I really don't know. I'm open to suggestions on this one, guys. We've spoken to everyone involved at the time, and nothing. I really can't see what else we can do."

"I agree," Joanna said. "Usually, we have a hint of something we can delve into by now, but not on this case. I feel a failure and I hate feeling this way."

Sally shook her head. "None of us should feel that way, Joanna. If the clues aren't there, then there is very little we can do about it. We've checked the database, covered our arses there. At the time of Millie's death, there weren't any other similar deaths on record. The man who did this could be dead by now for all we know."

"True enough. Maybe he did the right thing and killed himself after taking Millie's life. It's frustrating all the same, the not knowing."

"I'll second that," Joanna said, staring at her computer screen.

"Guys, let's not get downhearted over this. Yes, it's frustrating, but then so are all our cases at the beginning, usually until something slots into place. Let's call it a day for now and come back tomorrow, revitalised and ready for action, agreed?"

Jack shrugged, and Joanna nodded then switched off her computer. "What about Stuart and Jordan?"

The door barged open, and in walked the two men.

"Someone mention our names?" Stuart asked smugly.

"Good to see you, boys. How did you get on?"

Jack leapt out of his chair and bought the two men a coffee.

Stuart acted as the spokesperson and ran through what had gone on during the afternoon. "He's a decent enough chap. Didn't get the impression he was pulling a fast one on us at all. He teared up every time his wife's name was mentioned."

"That doesn't mean anything. It could be guilt, mate," Jack interrupted.

"Ever the pessimist, Jack. I've got two words to say to you: Craig Gillan," Sally shot at him.

Jack held his hands up. "All right, just stating facts. These guys have time to think when they're thrown in a cell. Maybe it's a case of him trying to fool you by giving off the signals he thinks will make the most impact. Did that even make sense?" he asked, frowning as if he'd confused himself.

Sally laughed. "I think we understood you, partner. It's definitely home time, guys. I'll put my thinking cap on and decide what to do next on both cases. Get some rest."

The team said their goodbyes and left Sally tidying the paperwork in her office. She felt despondent for the first time in ages as she drove home that evening. Simon was busy preparing the dinner when she entered the house.

He greeted her at the doorway to the kitchen. "Oh dear, bad day?"

He held out his arms, and she walked into them. He kissed the top of her head.

"How did you guess?"

"A nice glass of wine will drive away the workday blues, I guarantee it."

She glanced up at him and smiled. "Let's hope you're right."

He poured them both a glass of Sauvignon Blanc and returned to preparing the meal. "I thought I'd make chicken kievs tonight."

"Sounds delicious, can I help?"

"Nope, you sit there and keep me company."

Which sounded like a great idea to her. "How did your day pan out?"

"Today was a bit of a chore if I'm honest, going back to work. It's been really great spending the past few days with your father. I think we're going to make a brilliant team. He's far more knowledgeable about houses than I first gave him credit for. Don't tell him I said that, though."

Sally laughed. "You two make a superb team. There was never any doubt about that, love. I guess you have your answer about whether to throw in the towel at your day job or not then."

"I think you're right. Okay, enough about our business. Why the glum face when you walked in?"

"Sorry, I didn't mean for you to see that. It's been a super frustrating day, and we're struggling as a team to get this case started."

"Can I help at all?"

"Not really. You've looked into the original PM for me and found nothing. I'm not sure what else you can do without any evidence to go over."

"I feel your frustration on this one, love."

"Maybe have another look over the reports for me. If nothing comes from that, then we're going to have to close the case again. I hate being a defeatist, you know that…"

He crossed the kitchen and pecked her on the cheek. "I know. Hey, it's not often you give up on a case, Sal. Try not to be too down about it."

"I think I feel worse about this one because of the age of the victim. She had her whole life ahead of her. Everyone keeps telling me what a precious and adorable child she was. Oh, by the way, Jack and I went to see her brother today. Man, that was a tough visit on all of us."

"I can only imagine. Is he still cut up about her death?"

"Yes, although he's managed to push it aside a little. He's married now, and his wife is expecting their first child in a couple of months."

"That's brilliant news. I'm sure having the baby around will help with the healing process."

"Maybe. Only time will tell. How long before dinner?"

"A good ten minutes."

"I'm going to take a quick shower and get changed then, if that's all right?"

"Of course, it's a shame I haven't got time to join you."

"Cheeky."

6

Friday came and went. It proved to be far longer than Sally anticipated. The team worked hard all day, sitting down in a huddle, going over every minute detail of the Pickrel case. At lunchtime, Sally decided to send Stuart and Jordan out to question Lucinda Barratt's friends and work colleagues. That left her, Jack and Joanna discussing the Pickrel case. As promised, Simon rang mid-afternoon after he'd had a chance to go through the post-mortem results a second time in as many days.

"Hi, anything for me?" she asked.

"To add to your woes, nothing from what I can tell. The child died of asphyxiation. The original pathologist noted that the death was slightly prolonged, however."

"Prolonged? Meaning?"

"I took it to mean that the person doing the suffocating possibly hesitated. Maybe he had a moral issue with what he was doing. Or it could mean that the boy interrupted him, and the intruder pushed down harder to finish the girl off?" Simon suggested.

"There's a thought. Hang on, Louie said that he shouted at the man and he instantly bolted, as far as I can recall."

"Maybe he did. I don't know what the sequence of events was. All I know is what's in front of me."

"Thanks, Simon. Can you do me a favour and send me that report? I don't seem to have it in my damn file."

"Sure. I'll email it to you within the next ten minutes. See you later."

"You're a darling." She blew a kiss down the line and hung up.

"Eew…can you leave the lovey-dovey stuff at home next time?" Jack complained from the doorway to her office.

"That'll teach you to eavesdrop. Simon thinks he's found something of interest in the PM report. He's sending it through in the next ten minutes."

"Interesting how?"

"About the time it took for the child to die…poor thing suffered a prolonged death."

Jack frowned. "Is that so remarkable? Isn't suffocation quite a lengthy death compared to other methods?"

"Maybe. Oh, I don't know, maybe it's a hopeless attempt on my part to get this damn case started. Let's face it, we've got very little else to go on."

"Hmm… You're right. It could turn out to be something important. Best not to discount it yet."

She turned to look out of the window, peered up at the sky.

"Something wrong?" he asked, following her gaze.

"I'm searching for that notorious flying pig. Jesus, I can't believe you agreed with me for a change."

He shrugged, turned to walk away and threw over his shoulder, "It was a one-off. Don't get used to it."

Sally laughed, screwed up a piece of paper and aimed it at his retreating back. She caught him on the base of his neck.

"Now that's a miracle," he called out, "you hitting the target like that."

She didn't have the heart to tell him that she was actually aiming at his backside.

The afternoon dragged by. At five o'clock, she ordered the team to go home and enjoy their weekend, which was what she intended to do.

Sally and Simon cleaned the house together on Saturday morning and then picked Dex up from her parents and took him for a long walk down by the river. He was always exuberant in their company. Her heart lurched when she saw him, his tail wagging nonstop.

Lorne was eager to see Dex and insisted they bring him with them to the barbecue the following day. Sally was super excited to catch up with her best friend and found it difficult to sleep on Saturday. Her lack of sleep didn't make her grumpy the following day, though. She showered, took Dex for another long walk at sunrise and returned home to find Simon preparing a healthy fresh fruit salad for breakfast.

"I thought about doing a fry-up for a few seconds; decided on going for the healthy option instead."

"Great minds. I was going to do the very same thing when I got back. I hope I didn't keep you awake last night?"

"Not really. You know me, once I'm asleep, a herd of cattle couldn't disturb me. Do we have to take anything with us?"

"I bought a couple of bottles of wine and two of those salted caramel cheesecakes we love."

"Sounds good to me. You needn't have bought the wine. I could have raided the wine cellar. This auspicious occasion deserves the best wine possible."

Her eyes widened. "It's a barbecue, Si, not a state dinner."

He waved a hand at her. "It's a 'welcome to the area' party for your friends."

"You win, hey, they're your friends, too, now."

"Sorry, I know that. Come on, eat up, I'm eager to see their faces when we tell them we're going to be neighbours."

"Can I be the one to tell them?"

He flung an arm around her shoulder and pulled her in for a hug. "Of course. I'd never step on your toes with something like this."

They ate their breakfast, and while Sally washed up the dishes, Simon put Dex in the car.

"I'll be two minutes. Don't forget to sort out a couple of bottles of wine," she reminded him.

"No fear of that."

7

Sally's heart was pounding rapidly as Simon brought the car to a stop on the large sweeping drive that was dotted with weeds.

Lorne ran across the gravel and squeezed Sally so tightly she struggled to breathe. "Oh my God, can you believe we're here? It's wonderful to see you. I've missed you so much."

"Any chance of you allowing me to breathe?" Sally asked, laughing.

"Sorry. I'm a tad excited. Where's the boy?" Lorne peered into the back of the car.

Dex barked excitedly.

Simon stepped out of his car and into Lorne's waiting arms. "Good to see you again, Lorne."

"You, too, Simon. Can I get Dex out?"

"Go for it."

Lorne opened the back of the Range Rover and bent to kiss Dex on the tip of his nose. "Hey, boy, welcome to the madhouse."

Dex complained noisily but wagged his tail nevertheless.

"Talkative soul, aren't you?" Lorne ruffled his head.

"Always been the same. I'm dying to meet Sheba and the rest of the dogs. Have they all settled into their new home?"

"They have. I'm surprised it hasn't taken them longer. The grounds are fantastic, secure, which we weren't expecting, so no work to be done on that score for a change. You'll see what I mean when we venture out the back. Enough about us, how are you? You look tired, and the sparkle is missing from those beautiful eyes of yours. Is everything all right?"

"I won't bore you with the details now. It's work-related, and today is supposed to be about us all catching up and having some fun."

"Hear, hear," Tony shouted, making his way towards them. "Come on, let's have a drink and then do a tour of the place."

Tony and Simon carried the wine and the cheesecakes into the house ahead of Lorne and Sally.

Lorne linked arms with her. "I meant what I said, it's fabulous to see you. Can't believe we're living so close to each other now."

You'll hit another stratosphere when you learn the truth.

"We're going to have so much fun. Time for both of us to start living our lives the way they should be lived, eh?"

"Definitely. I'm loving my retirement already. I have to say, I haven't missed work at all." They walked through the dated hallway. "Ignore the décor, it's all going to be changed once we're settled. I can't wait to get stuck in."

Sally laughed. "Same old Lorne, always thinking of the next adventure. You're supposed to be taking it easy, remember?"

Lorne placed a hand over the wound in her stomach, the result of a knife attack a few months earlier. "I'm healing nicely, don't worry about me." She leaned in close and whispered, "I've already started drawing up the plans for the renovations I'd like to have done soon. Don't tell Tony, though."

"You're incorrigible. You've got all the time in the world to think about that, at least get the unpacking out of the way first, although, if I were you, I'd be tempted to ignore the unpacking and give the renovations priority."

Lorne placed a finger against her flushed cheek. "Now there's a thought. Do you know any good builders?"

They both roared with laughter.

"What's so funny?" Simon asked, eyeing them up curiously.

"Lorne just asked if I can recommend a good builder."

And that's how the day continued, full of laughter, good food and excellent wine. A day to remember for years to come. After their meat-filled barbecue and their indulgent pudding was out of the way, the four of them decided to let the dogs out of the kennels and go for a walk around the grounds. Dex and Sheba play-fought with the other dogs which had them all in fits of laughter. It was a joy to see them all running free.

"This is where our land ends," Lorne announced, pointing to the hedgerow.

"Hmm...it's quite an area you have here. I'd consider putting a gate in there, however." Sally bubbled with excitement inside.

Lorne's brow furrowed. "Are you mad? Why would I want to do that? The damn neighbours would probably traipse in and out all day long if we did that."

"Is there a problem with that?" Sally asked, trying her very best to keep a straight face.

Simon coughed behind her. She glanced in his direction. He nodded for her to go ahead.

"Why do I sense we're in the dark about something here? Spill, missus," Lorne ordered, her eyes narrowing.

"I thought it might be a good idea to have access to next door, you know, in case there's an emergency."

Lorne shook her head. "I don't really do chatting over the fence with a neighbour. Tony and I prefer our own company in that respect. So, I'll be buggered if I'm going to put a damn gate in. Anyway, I have the dogs to consider."

"That's right, you have. And Dex would love the chance to play with his new doggy friends."

Lorne scratched her head. "You seriously need a holiday of sorts,

Sal, you're talking gobbledygook. The sooner the better would be my advice."

"Ah, that's not likely to happen in the near future," Sally replied, her heart pounding.

"Why? Because of this case you've been working on?"

Sally shook her head, tugged Lorne to the side until the house next door came into view and pointed. "Nice house."

"It is. Another reason we'll be keeping ourselves to ourselves. Can you imagine the kind of snobs who live in a place as grand as that?"

Simon snorted, and Sally tipped her head back, laughing until the tears cascaded down her cheeks. She grabbed Lorne and hugged her tightly. Pulling back, she studied her friend's bewildered face. "They're nice people." Sally reached for Simon's hand. He walked towards her and stood beside her, their hands clasped tightly together. "I don't think they're snobs at all. In fact, I hear they're newlyweds."

Realisation suddenly dawned on Lorne's face, and she gasped. "No way! No *frigging* way! You haven't?"

"Wait a minute, what the hell is everyone talking about?" Tony asked, his gaze drifting between the others.

"Don't you see, Tony? Simon and Sally are our new neighbours."

"Bloody hell. Is this a joke?" Tony asked Simon.

He shook his head. "Straight up, mate. I picked the house up at the auction this week."

Lorne did something that surprised them all then. She turned away and performed a perfect cartwheel. "Yippee, yip, yip. I can't believe it. This is the best news ever." She stood erect and placed a hand on her wound. "Ouch! Maybe that wasn't the best way to celebrate the news."

All the dogs seemed to sense their enjoyment. They took off back to the house, barking and toppling over each other as they ran.

Sally and Simon were forced to get a taxi home that night as the celebrations went on into the early hours of the morning. Simon told Lorne he'd pick the car up the following day, sometime in the afternoon.

Sally arrived at work feeling more than a little fragile, and her head pounded as the taxi dropped her off at the station. She wasn't keen on risking her licence and would cadge a lift from Jack after their shift ended, and if he didn't feel like obliging, Simon could come out and pick her up.

"Good Lord, you didn't drive into work in that state, did you?" Jack asked, the second he laid eyes on her. "You look rougher than a badger's arse."

"That bad, eh? And do you mind not shouting, I'm feeling a little brittle today."

"Copious cups of coffee on the agenda this morning then, I take it."

"Thanks for offering," she said, gingerly heading for her office, hoping against hope the postal gods were smiling on her and her desk was relatively clear. She cautiously poked her head into the office and groaned. "No such luck." She entered the room, placed her handbag on the floor and dropped into her chair. She opened her drawer and extracted a packet of Nurofen. Even removing the tablets from their plastic packaging grated on her delicate nerves.

Jack joined her and placed two coffees on her desk. "Looks like you could do with a double whammy first thing. How come you're in this self-inflicted state? A celebration, was it? Tell me to mind my own business if you want," he added, not pausing long enough for her to chip in with an answer.

Her brain rattled against her skull. "Rewind, sorry, what was your first question again?"

"Jesus. I don't recall ever getting in the state you're in, not the day before I was due back to work anyway."

Sally raised a hand to stop him. "I can do without the lecture, partner."

He stormed out of the office.

Damn, bang goes my lift home tonight. She drank the first coffee without it even touching the sides, even though it was still relatively hot. Then she tackled the first of the brown envelopes on her desk.

Thirty minutes later, the caffeine had done a remarkable job of making her feel near normal again, and she left the office.

Joanna was on the phone, concern etched into her features. She glanced in Sally's direction. Sally crossed the room, ignoring her partner's scowling and perched herself on the desk closest to Joanna.

"What's up?" she mouthed.

"Hold the line a sec, Sergeant, DI Parker wants a word."

Joanna passed the phone over, and Sally shrugged.

"Sergeant who?" she asked, covering the phone.

"Sorry, boss. It's Sergeant Sullivan. You'll want to speak to him. I was just about to patch the call through to you."

Sally had an ominous tingling running the length of her spine. "Pat, it's Sally. What's going on?"

"Sorry to interrupt you, ma'am, you know me, always got my ear to the ground. Well, something happened overnight that you should be aware of. It might not be related; I'm probably thinking it is without really thinking about it, in fact."

"You're waffling, Pat, you know I hate wafflers. Get to the point, man."

He gulped noisily. "It's probably nothing. I know you're working on a cold case at the moment. Well, something was reported last night and…"

"You got my attention at the beginning of this conversation, Pat. Don't let it wander, get to the point, please?"

He heaved out a sigh. "Sorry, this one has shaken me to the core. Okay, there was an incident that took place. An intruder entered a house and killed a child. Smothered her with a pillow, they did."

Sally closed her eyes and shook her head. "Fuck. Excuse my language. Okay, I can understand why it's upset you so much. Who's the SIO?"

"Brian Jessop. He's new around here. Want me to see if he'll drop by and see you?"

"You read my mind, Pat. ASAP, if you will. It could be a coincidence."

"Neither you nor I believe in such things, do we, Inspector? I'll get on to him now. I hope I haven't spoken out of turn, ma'am?"

"Not as far as I'm concerned, Pat. Any information you've

supplied in the past on a case has always been worth chasing up. I appreciate you contacting me regarding this one."

"I'll get in touch with Jessop now, ma'am."

Sally ended the call and handed the phone back to Joanna. "Shit. I take it you got the gist of that?" she asked the other members of the team who were all staring at her. "As Pat just said, we don't believe in coincidences. I hope for our sakes I'm wrong in this instance. If not, it means the killer has bloody resurfaced."

8

*J*ack threw his pen across the desk and covered his face with his hands then slid them through his hair and onto the top of his head. "No frigging way! We can't say that yet, boss, it's too soon to speculate something like that."

"Let's hold fire on speculation until we've got the confirmed facts from the SIO. Pat's getting on to him, to see if he'll drop by and see me. I'll leave it until midday. If he hasn't made contact by then, I'll chase him up."

No sooner had she told the team that, than the door burst open and a young suited man entered the room. His hair was slicked back with a severe amount of gel. His face contorted in what Sally read as anger stroke confusion.

"Who's in charge around here?"

Sally left the desk she was perched on and offered her outstretched hand. "That would be me, DI Sally Parker. Am I right in thinking you're Brian Jessop?"

"Yes, I'm a sergeant."

"Thanks for clearing that up, Sergeant. Do you want to take a seat in my office?"

"Here will do."

Sally glanced past him at Jack who was making the sign that he thought Jessop was a dickhead. She suppressed the laugh threatening to emerge and invited the sergeant to take a seat.

He declined. "I've been instructed by the desk sergeant to come and see you. Something about a cold case you're working on."

"Pat believes there is a similarity between the case you're working on and the one we're investigating."

"You're not having it."

Sally frowned and tilted her head. "Excuse me? Having what?"

"My case."

"Did I mention anything about taking over your investigation?" she snapped back. Jessop's churlish behaviour was prodding her annoyance gene with a very large stick.

"It's my first real case. You might think I'm still wet behind the ears, but I'll fight you every step of the way on this one."

Jack got to his feet and approached the sergeant.

Sally held up a hand. "Jack, it's okay."

"I ain't gonna stand by and let a pipsqueak like him talk to you like that."

"I can handle it, partner. Sit down," she replied.

All this time Jessop ignored Jack, his gaze remaining firmly focused on Sally. "I won't be intimidated either."

Sally rolled her eyes. "Why don't you try and calm down, take a seat, and we'll discuss this like adults?"

He huffed out a breath and dropped into a chair.

"Jack, can you get Mr Jessop a coffee?"

Jack left his seat, strode past her and muttered, "If I must."

"Black for me," Jessop shouted.

His abruptness didn't recede at all over the next ten minutes as Sally ran through the Pickrel case with him. "I don't get it. Still not sure why you asked me to come and see you when I'm chocka with a new case."

Sally shook her head, which was now clear of the alcohol she'd consumed the previous day. Jack muttered something again. Sally glared at her partner and pulled an imaginary zip across her lips. "Don't you see? It's the same MO."

Jessop blew out an exasperated breath. "Is it? Really? Almost twenty years apart?"

"I know it sounds like I'm building my hopes up on this one, but I think we should work together on this case, both cases. Are you up for that?"

"Honestly? No. I'm not relinquishing my hold on this case, whether you're a senior officer or not, ma'am." The 'ma'am' was said through gritted teeth.

Sally saw Jack fidgeting in his chair out of her peripheral vision. She shot her partner a warning glance.

"Why the hostility, Sergeant Jessop? Don't you want to pool our resources? Not even for the families' sakes?"

"Not really, no. This is my chance to hit the big time. If I can solve this case, then I can see a bright future ahead of me and a swift climb up the promotional ladder."

Jack growled. Sally shot him another warning glance.

"While I admire your ambition, that's not the way the force works, Brian. Is it all right if I call you Brian?"

"I don't mind. Can I call you Sally?" he asked, smirking.

You're a tosser, man. One who needs to be put in his place.

"No, I'm your senior officer. I've earned the respect of my colleagues over the years because of the cases I've solved and the promotions I've achieved through my extremely hard work. For your information, I've solved around fifty cases throughout my career so far. Going by what you've just said about your own ambitions, I reckon I should be ranked a commander by now."

"Maybe your gender has gone against you on that score, Inspector."

"Possibly. I do wonder if that's the truth sometimes. Anyway, we've veered off the subject slightly. Look, I'm willing to let you take the credit for solving your case. I have never said otherwise. What do you say? Shall we try and figure this out together?"

He shook his head slowly. "I can't do that, ma'am. My DI wouldn't accept it."

"What if I clear it with your DI first, how about that?"

He sat and chewed his bottom lip for a while. "You could ask. I'd still feel awkward about working alongside you."

"May I ask why?"

He shrugged. "I can't put my finger on it. I just don't see how combining the two cases is going to get us anywhere."

Sally had heard enough. She leaned back and took out her notebook. "What's the name of your DI?"

"DI James Wagstaff. He's a tough man to get around, ma'am, just warning you."

Sally entered her office and contacted Wagstaff. Once she'd explained the situation to him, he agreed that it would be better if they worked together.

"Will you tell Jessop that or shall I?" she enquired.

"I'm granting you permission to do it."

"Coward."

Wagstaff laughed. "He means well, Sally. Eager pup syndrome. Be gentle with him."

Sally's mood lightened. "Gee, thanks, James. I'll send him back to you once I've chewed his balls off."

"I'm glad I'm not in his position."

"Any hassle from him, and I'll come after your gonads, matey."

"Ouch! I hear you." Wagstaff ended the call.

Sally left her desk and returned to find the team and Jessop sitting in silence. Which didn't bode well if the team was expected to welcome Jessop into their investigation. She smiled as Jessop faced her. "Looks like we're gonna share the case, Brian. DI Wagstaff is of the same opinion as me. It would be unprofessional of us not to link the cases, whether there is a nineteen-year gap between the crimes or not."

"Great. Not what I was expecting to be confronted with when I travelled into work this morning. We'd better make the most of it then. I'm going out to the scene. Do you want to tag along?"

"I'm willing to let you take the lead on that one, if I can trust you to share the information with us?"

"I'm not one for not following instructions, Inspector. If DI Wagstaff has ordered me to liaise with you, then so be it."

"Maybe you should tag along, boss," Joanna piped up.

Sally weighed the decision up for a second or two, the fact that they'd been grappling around searching for clues at the end of the previous week prominent in her mind. "Okay, I think Joanna is right. I'll come to the scene with you. You can fill me in on the details en route. I take it you want to get over there ASAP?"

"I was about to leave when I was instructed to come and see you. It's up to you if you want to come or not, but I'm leaving now."

"Give me two minutes to instruct my team. I'll meet you in the car park."

"Mine's the silver Beemer," he replied smugly.

"See you soon." She dismissed the man then turned her attention to her team. "I don't have to tell you what to do, guys, on this new case. See if anything shows up regarding the inhabitants at the address et cetera."

"One suggestion, boss, if I may?" Joanna asked.

"Shoot."

"The address. It's roughly in the same area. If I were to put pins in a map, I'm sure all those people we've recently spoken to would live within a ten-mile radius of the crime."

"Definitely worth considering. Well spotted, Joanna. Are you all right, Jack?" She noted he was sitting in his seat, arms folded, straining the fabric on his suit, wearing a thunderous expression.

"Not really, but the decision has already been made."

"Meaning?"

"You're gonna have a new partner for the foreseeable future. So where does that leave me?"

Sally rolled her eyes and stroked a hand across her face. "It means nothing of the sort. You really think I'm up for spending time with that sourpuss? Although it'll make a pleasant change from spending time with my normal sourpuss." She grinned at him, trying her best to cut through the atmosphere he'd created.

He glared at her. "Sorry, am I supposed to laugh at this point?"

Sally shook her head. "Partner, you can do what you like. I'm off. You're in charge while I'm gone. Stop sulking, you have work to do."

"For your information, I am *not* sulking. I'm concerned."

"And I appreciate you showing your concern in such a forceful way, Jack." She smiled tautly at him.

He retorted with his usual childish answer, something he'd picked up from his kids, no doubt. "Whatever."

Not wishing to argue the toss further with him, she collected her bag from the office and left. Jessop was waiting in his car for her at the entrance. She hopped in. "Nice car."

"Thanks. I don't have a significant other or kids so I can afford to be extravagant and treat myself now and again. I've only had her a few months. Purrs along nicely as you'll discover soon enough."

"It's nice when we can treat ourselves; I don't blame you in the slightest."

The conversation dried up after that. It was obvious that Brian Jessop was one of those men who preferred to talk about himself all day long. Was it any wonder he was single? He probably bored any potential girlfriends within thirty minutes of meeting them.

Sally never thought she'd be telling herself she was better off having Jack as a partner, but compared to Brian, Jack was a thousand times better.

The journey eventually ended at the crime scene. She was surprised to see the young family lived in a bungalow. The parents were in the lounge, the husband comforting his sobbing wife. Sally decided to hang back with any questions she had, leaving Brian to interview the parents. She regretted her decision once he started his line of enquiries using the same abrupt tone he'd used on her before she'd rung his superior.

"What time did the incident occur?" he demanded.

"We'd gone to bed around eleven, sometime between then and two. Our son was crying; he shared the same room as our daughter. I went to check on him and that's when I found the pillow over her..." Mrs Kilpatrick said, tears falling as she spoke.

"It's all right, love, take your time," her husband consoled her. "What my wife was trying to say is she found our daughter with the pillow over her...face and the bedroom window wide open."

"We're sorry to have to do this right now, Mr and Mrs Kilpatrick, I'm sure you understand the reasons behind that. Please, if you're finding this too difficult, we can stop at any time," Sally interjected swiftly, not giving Brian another chance to fire more questions at the couple without any thought for their feelings.

Brian shot her a glance, his eyes narrowed with anger.

She smiled at him. "Sorry, DS Jessop, carry on."

"Thank you." He faced the couple again and, his expression appearing to soften a little, he asked, "Did you hear anything? Was the window open when you went to bed?"

"Yes, we always leave the window open a little. We won't in the future. That won't help Holly, though," the father said. "No, my wife and I were both asleep."

"How old is your son?" Sally interrupted again.

"He's four, our daughter was seven. Oh God, can she really be gone? At such a young age? I can't believe it." He buried his head in his shaking hands.

His wife leaned her head into him, and he hugged her.

Sally's heart broke in two watching the distraught couple deal with their grief, knowing there was no easy fix for something as traumatic as losing a child at such a young age. Anna and Louie Pickrel were testament to that. Brian went to ask something else. Sally touched his arm, and when he looked at her, she shook her head, telling him to give the parents a moment's respite.

He turned away and walked over to the window where he peered out at the other houses. Sally figured he was sizing up if any of the neighbours had a perfect view of the bungalow. In her book, it wouldn't really matter unless the children's bedroom was at the front.

"Where are the bedrooms, front or rear of the house?" she asked gently.

"At the rear," the father replied.

Brian left the window and stood beside Sally once more. "I have to ask the most obvious question: have you noticed anyone lurking on the estate recently?" Brian asked.

The couple glanced at each other and shook their heads.

"What about visitors? Has anyone visited the house, a tradesman for instance, in the past month or so?" Sally jumped in again.

"No, no one at all. Why, do you think the person who did this picked on us? Chose to kill our child?"

Sally shook her head. "It's far too soon to establish that, Mr Kilpatrick. We hope to have some clear and insightful answers for you soon. Is there anything else you think we should know?"

He shook his head. "No, nothing."

"What about relatives? Have you fallen out with any relatives or friends lately?" Sally asked.

"No, not at all. None of our friends or family could ever be responsible for something as horrific as this," Mr Kilpatrick snapped, clearly upset by the notion.

"Sorry, I had to ask," she replied.

"How long have you lived here?" Brian asked.

"Three years. We moved not long after our son was born."

"Did your son see anything? You said he woke you up and you heard him crying," Brian said.

"He said a man was in the room," Mrs Kilpatrick sniffled.

"Could he describe this man?" Brian pressed.

"I don't know. I think he'd be too traumatised," the husband answered.

"Where is your son now?"

"In our bedroom; he's asleep. We called the police and the ambulance at two. He's been awake since then, only dropped off an hour or so ago. You can't be considering asking him any questions," Mrs Kilpatrick announced, horrified.

"No. We wouldn't do that, not unless you were present anyway," Sally replied quickly.

Brian turned to look at her. She shrugged. It was true. What could a child of four tell them anyway?

"We'll leave you for now and go and question the neighbours. Again, we're truly sorry for your loss and want to assure you that we'll do our very best to bring the person responsible to justice." Sally left the room with Brian close on her heels.

Outside the bungalow, he pulled on her arm. "We agreed I'd be in charge of this investigation. I wasn't done in there."

Sally peered behind him, ensuring the front door was closed. "When you've quite finished having a hissing fit… You were too abrupt. I had to intervene. These people are grieving. Where's your compassion, man?"

He hung his head in shame. "I know. I'm doing my best to catch a suspect. I can't do that without their assistance, can I?"

"Granted, we're both trying to achieve the same result—not like that, though. You were firing the questions at them as if you were interrogating them. May I remind you that they're the innocent parties in all this? They've just lost their child, for fuck's sake."

"I'm sorry. I was in the wrong. Do you want me to go back in there and apologise?"

"No, leave it for now. We have work to do. We need to question all the neighbours. Anything they likely saw will go a long way to help us solving this case. You have to set aside the parents at this point in an investigation of this ilk. They're too close to the victim; their answers are likely to be blurry at best."

"I appreciate that now. Again, I apologise, I've never dealt with a child murder before."

"That's okay, we all have to learn somewhere. Just rein in your enthusiasm, put yourself in their shoes. If you had a visit from the police regarding the death of one of your relatives, think about what state of mind you'd be in."

"I get that. I can't keep apologising to you."

"I'm not asking you to. Anyway, it's not me you should be apologising to, it's them. Let's draw a line under this for now and press on. If you're unsure how to handle things in the field, you need to ask for guidance from those accompanying you at the scene." Sally began walking towards the first neighbour's house. She paused outside the gate to the bungalow next door.

"Thanks for the advice. Half the time I'm out here alone, so your advice doesn't really count."

"Are you kidding me?"

"Nope. It's the cuts. That's what they're always enforcing upon us anyway. I noticed how many members of staff you had on your team today and I have to say I was flabbergasted."

"We're lucky; however, we work hard. You know the history behind the cold case team being set up, right?" He shook his head. "One DI screwed up on several cases. Because of the dubious nature of his findings, we've been tasked to check all the cases he ever dealt with and the convictions pertaining to those investigations. What we're discovering would blow your mind. We've already released several people from prison who were incarcerated wrongly. I know this case is different, no one has been convicted in the past, but we're aiming to remedy that. Now your case could be connected—how, we've yet to find out. My team is all about righting the wrongs of an inspector who didn't care enough about his job. Don't be guilty of being like him, Brian. You're a bright young man. Take the time to think things through properly before jumping in and getting your feet wet. Okay?"

"Thanks for the pep talk. I'll try and do better in the future."

She patted his arm. "That's a start. Shall we split up, or do you want to watch me do the first one and split up after that?"

"If you don't mind, that'd be great."

She smiled. "It's my pleasure. Come on then, time's a wasting, and we have a killer to catch." Sally opened the gate to a neatly presented bungalow. She was guessing by the way the pristine garden was exhibited that she was about to find elderly neighbours in residence.

The ring on the bell was answered promptly by a man in his sixties who greeted them warily. "Hello, what can I do for you? I'm taking it that you're the police?"

"You'd be correct, sir." Sally showed her ID and introduced herself and Brian. "Would it be okay if we came in for a brief chat?"

The man peered up at the grey sky. "I should, it's going to piss down soon. Shut the door behind you, laddie."

Sally grinned at Brian, and they both entered the house. The man turned left into a large living room that stretched to the back of the house. The garden at the rear was equally as well-maintained as the front.

"Don't stand on ceremony, take a seat now."

Sally sat on one end of the Dralon couch while Brian sat on the other, his notebook finally emerging from his pocket. "I didn't catch your name, sir?"

"I'm not surprised, I haven't told you what it is yet. I'm Donald Cotton. I've lived here twenty-odd years and have never had the police on my doorstep, not until today. All this is quite unnerving, I have to say."

"We appreciate that, sir. It's tragic circumstances that bring us here."

"It is. I'm aware of what has happened to the child. Absolutely deplorable that someone should enter the house and intentionally do that to a youngster. Whatever possesses someone to do such a thing?"

"We can't answer that, not yet, not until we find the person who committed the crime, sir. Did you either hear or see anything last night?"

"I heard the screams of the poor mother, Jessica. That sound will remain with me forever. No parent should be subjected to such an ordeal. To know that your child was killed while you were in the next room, asleep in your own bed. Jesus, they must both be devastated. I haven't seen them yet, thought I'd give them a bit of space."

"They'll appreciate you for being so considerate. They're distraught by what's happened. So, am I right in thinking that you didn't see a stranger lurking on the close last night?"

"No. I'm not one of these people who stand at their window spying on their neighbours at all hours, I'm sorry to say. Wish I was now; perhaps I could have stopped the bastard. Do you know what time the person entered the house?"

"We believe it was sometime around two this morning."

"Bugger! I doubt many folks around here will be able to help you. We have a good community spirit amongst us, we all look out for each other. I assure you, if anyone had been hanging around here then someone would have done the right thing and rung the police. We don't take no shit, if you get what I mean?"

"I do. You're the first person we've interviewed. Hopefully someone else will be able to help us then."

"That is if there was an intruder in the first place," he said, raising his eyebrows.

"Are you suggesting one of the parents might have committed the crime, sir? Killed their own child?" Sally was taken aback by the suggestion. She'd been so focused about matching the two cases that she'd blocked out any other possible scenarios.

"Who knows? There's so much anger around these days, isn't there? I hear the mother shouting at the children all day long. I bought this bungalow expecting the residents to be elderly like myself. They're the only youngsters on the close and, well…sometimes they drive the rest of us to distraction."

"Oh my, terribly sorry to hear that."

"Don't be. There's one less to worry about now. Maybe that'll put an end to all the screeching we have to listen to every day."

Sally winced at his words. Surely, he hadn't meant for his statement to sound so heartless. "Do the other residents feel the same way as you do?"

"Some do, some are too deaf to hear all the damn noise, lucky buggers. There are days when I curse my good hearing. There's something about a kid's scream that puts your teeth on edge, wouldn't you agree?"

She sighed heavily. She wasn't sure how to take this man. Was he just airing his grievances with her while the opportunity was open to him? Or could what he'd told them be taken as the truth and viable information for the investigation? Sally had a feeling the former option was at play here. "Can't say I've really noticed that myself. Is there anything else you think we should know regarding the family? For instance, have you ever witnessed the parents hitting either of the children?"

His eyes narrowed as he thought. "Nope, nothing like that. I'm sure most parents get tempted these days, don't they? What with their kids being far more unruly than in my day. I blame all these damn computer games. A lot of them are noisy and kill people from what I can gather."

The old man had a point. She knew there was always some form of research going on, probing into whether the use of these types of games had a detrimental effect on people's character. Maybe they were to blame for the way children, and adults who played them for that matter, reacted to things in normal life. But would someone intentionally go out and kill a child because of a game?

Sally rose from her seat, and Brian followed.

The man seemed surprised. "You're not going, are you?"

"We have to question the other neighbours, sir. Thank you for seeing us today."

"That's the trouble these days, everyone is in such a hurry. I'm sorry you feel this conversation has been a waste of time."

"Now you're simply putting words in my mouth. As I've said, there's just the two of us and we have to speak to the other neighbours quickly if we're going to catch the culprit. Thank you for sparing us some of your valuable time, sir."

He humphed as he got out of his chair and showed them to the front door. "Old Bob over there, he tends to be up until the early hours of the morning. He suffers from that insomnia." He pointed at one of the bungalows opposite.

"That's very informative. Thank you for your help."

"Just catch the bastard. We need to feel safe in our own homes."

"We're going to do our best," Sally called over her shoulder.

Brian closed the gate behind him; they were still under the watchful gaze of Donald Cotton. Her temporary partner leaned in close. "I thought you handled him well. I think I would've lost my rag with him not long after the conversation started."

"Thanks. You'll learn to be patient when trying to seek out the information you need. Let's split up. I'm going to see Bob next. Why don't you work your way along this side, and I'll continue on the other. Just ask the basic questions. Ask them predominantly if they saw anything last night, if so, what? At the end of the conversation, enquire what the family are like. Mr Cotton might have stumbled upon something there without realising it."

"You think?" He shrugged. "I suppose the parents might've seen the appeal go out recently from Anna Pickrel."

Sally tilted her head. "You could have something there, and they used the same excuse to kill their own child? I've got my team checking into the parents' backgrounds now. We'll see what surfaces there. Let's crack on. Don't hesitate to give me a shout if you need my advice on anything, not that I'm doubting your abilities."

"I'll be fine now I've seen you in action."

Sally smiled. "Good luck. We'll aim to get in and out quickly, but also be compassionate. Remember we're dealing with the death of a child here."

"I hear you." He set off to the right while Sally crossed the road and knocked on Bob's front door. She withdrew her notebook and waited for the resident to open it.

An elderly gentleman greeted her with a smile. "I saw you over at Donald's. Knew he'd send you my way."

Sally smiled. "Bob, is it? I'm DI Sally Parker. Mind if I come in for a brief chat?"

He stood behind the door and motioned for her to step into the hallway.

"Thank you."

"Anything to help the police. Come through to the kitchen, and I'll make you a cup of tea."

"That would be lovely, thank you, sir." She didn't have the heart to tell him she didn't drink tea and assumed he'd have coffee in the house, which was considered an extravagance to some old folks, so she'd heard.

"Terrible thing, what happened over the road. No doubt you'll be wanting to know what I heard and saw."

Sally flipped open her notebook and poised her pen. "It would make my life a lot easier if you told me you saw something, sir. Did you?"

He put a splash of milk into each cup along with a teabag. "Sugar?"

"Two please," she said, hoping the sugar would mask the taste of the tea.

The kettle finished boiling. He poured the water into the mugs and placed a spoon in each then walked across the room to the small kitchen table. "Take the weight off your feet and drink that. There's a saucer to put your teabag on when it's brewed."

"You're very kind. Did you see anything last night?"

He nodded. "I saw a man standing by the hedge around one, give or take ten minutes."

Her interest immediately piqued. "You did? Could you make him out? His features, height, build et cetera?"

He left the table and the room and returned carrying a slip of paper. "I took down all the details just in case he was up to no good. There was no point ringing your lot. I've done that before, and no one has bothered to come out."

"This is excellent," she replied, reading through his spidery scrawl, stumbling across certain words but then managing to figure out what they were in the context of the sentence. "I'm sorry you've been let down by us in the past. I'll look into that when I get back to the station."

"If you would. It's peace of mind we need at our age. No good ringing the police and reporting a possible crime if we're going to be ignored, is there?"

"I understand that, Bob. It won't happen again, I assure you. I take it you watched this man for a while?"

"I did. He must have stayed there about twenty minutes. I had to nip to the loo then. When I came back, he'd gone. I foolishly believed he'd got bored and buggered off. It wasn't until I saw all the commotion going on over at the Kilpatricks' that I realised he'd carried out his intentions."

"That's why you didn't make the call, because you thought he'd gone?"

"That and the fact I've been ignored before. No doubt my conscience would've driven me to ringing your lot eventually. I don't know how I feel about things now I've heard what the bastard did. I'm determined not to feel guilty but I've got a niggle in my gut." He placed his head in his hands.

Sally rubbed his arm. "Please don't punish yourself, none of this is your fault."

He dried his eyes on the sleeve of his woollen jumper. "But knowing I could have likely prevented it, well, that hurts more than any words can express."

"I understand, sir. I'd probably feel the same if I were in your shoes. You've given us a pretty good description of the man here. I have to ask, would you be willing to work with a police sketch artist to define his features?"

"I would. I'd like to help the poor parents in any way I can. I can't imagine the pain they're going through right now. Horrendous, it must be."

"I agree. Okay, let me make a quick call, get that organised." She picked up her mobile and rang the desk sergeant. "Pat, I'm out at the crime scene. I've got a possible witness who is willing to work with a sketch artist. Can you organise that for me?"

"I'll see if she's available. What address, ma'am?"

"Bob, what number are you?"

"Thirty."

Sally nodded her thanks. "It's number thirty, the bungalow opposite the Kilpatricks' place."

"Leave it with me. Want me to confirm a rendezvous time with yourself, ma'am?"

"If you would. Thanks, Pat." She gave the sergeant a brief description of the offender so he could issue an alert to his team, then she hung up and took a sip of her drink. "He should get back to me pretty soon."

"Do you think this has anything to do with that other case that was highlighted on the TV last week? Seems odd that someone should target a child in the same way. Of course, that's all presumption on my part as to what has gone on over there. I heard the mother's screams during the night when everyone should be tucked up in bed."

"First things first, we can't compare or connect the two crimes at present. It'll be there at the back of my mind, but we'll need to find some form of evidence before we can make that leap. And yes, the child was found in her bed, smothered with a pillow, so the similarities are there. Although we need to be cautious going forward. If we start off investigating the wrong line of enquiries, it could damage the current investigation."

"I get that. Once you've pieced it all together, what do you think the likelihood is?"

"Nice try. Honestly, I tend to work with the facts and evidence to hand. I'm never one to make assumptions. That could derail the case and would be foolish." Her phone rang. "Yes, Pat?"

"She can come out this afternoon, ma'am, at two, if that's acceptable?"

"Let me check." She covered the phone and asked, "Is two this afternoon okay for you, Bob?"

"I don't have any appointments this afternoon; yes, that's fine."

"Hi, Pat. That's an affirmative. Thanks for sorting that out for me. See you soon."

"You're welcome, ma'am."

Sally drank half her tea and decided to leave the rest. "I'll leave the sheet of paper here. You can refresh your memory before the sketch artist shows up." She took a photo and placed her phone back in her pocket.

He prodded his temple with his forefinger. "If you like, but it's all up here, along with the guilt."

"Please, there's no need for you to feel guilty. We have to think positive about this. If you hadn't spotted the man then we'd be running around chasing our tails right now. With your help, we'll be a lot further forward with the case and on the trail of a suspect soon enough."

"Unlike that other case, you mean?"

"It's a difficult one for sure. How the mother and son must feel after being in limbo for the past nineteen years, well, I can only imagine."

"Downright heartbreaking, it is. To think it happened nearly two decades ago, and there's no sign of a suspect."

"We're doing our best. Okay, I'm going to have to move on to the next neighbour now, Bob, unless there's anything else you'd like to tell me?"

"No, not really. I hope you manage to find this bastard, for the family's sake. I know they're close, they do the right thing by their children. Always seem to be going off on some sort of adventure at the weekends. They care about their children, unlike some parents nowadays who seem to kick them out on the street to disrupt the traffic on their bikes most days."

"That's good to hear. Donald was under the impression the family didn't really get on that well together."

"He's a grumpy old man at the best of times. Comes over here for a cuppa, and he's non-stop, running the neighbours down left, right and bloody centre, that one. I'd take what he says with a pinch of salt."

Sally smiled. "He even led me to believe the mother shouted at the children, hinted that he wouldn't put it past the parents killing the child."

Bob growled. "Seriously? He needs a kick up the arse, he does. Damn silly sod. His gaff should be known as Gossip Central. Always wittering on or slagging off someone if they've spoken out against him. You ask the others on the street, they'll tell you the same thing, I can guarantee it."

"I'll disregard what he said about the family then. Thanks for the drink, it was kind of you. Hope all goes well with the artist this afternoon. I wish there were more people like you around, it would make our job a whole lot easier."

"I like to do my best. I hope your case gets solved soon, both of them. You're to be admired taking on a current case and a cold case, that's for sure."

"Time will tell on that one." Sally left the house and glanced across the street at Brian who was jotting something down in his notebook.

He must have sensed her looking at him because he peered over his shoulder and raised a thumb in her direction.

She paused a few moments as he appeared to be finishing up speaking with the direct neighbour on the other side of the Kilpatricks. He trotted across the road to her.

"Any good?" she asked.

"Not really. She's one of those who are out for the count once their head hits the pillow. What about you?"

"I think I hit the jackpot. Trying to rein in my excitement, though. Bob saw a man lingering last night for around twenty minutes. He nipped to the loo and when he came back the man had gone. He presumed he'd got bored and moved on. Kicking himself for not calling us out."

"Damn, why didn't he?"

"He's called us before, and no one has bothered showing up, so he didn't see the point."

"Bloody hell, that's not the reputation we want, is it?"

"No, it's not. I'll be having a word once we get back to the station. He was pretty good at writing down the man's description. I've arranged for a sketch artist to drop by and see him this afternoon. Once we have that to hand, we can act on it. It's going to be a tough ask to solve this one without it. Why don't we rush through the other interviews and get back to base?"

"Sounds good to me. I'm dying for a cuppa."

Sally's guilt gene prodded her gut. "Another hour, okay?"

"Agreed."

They went their separate ways again and continued their enquiries on either side of the street. An hour later, every house had been covered. The occupants of the bungalows at the end of the road proved to be less informative than those living closer to the Kilpatricks. Nevertheless, everyone appeared to be in shock that a major crime had been committed.

Sally had done her best to calm their fears by telling them that she would be ensuring a patrol checked on the area regularly over the coming weeks. Sod the cuts, people's lives were at risk.

They travelled back to base. Upon their arrival, Sally had a brief chat with Pat, making him aware of the situation, about Bob's calls to the station being ignored in the past.

"Damn, not what we want to hear, ma'am. I'll look into that for you and pull someone over the coals if necessary."

"Thanks, Pat. I knew I could rely on you."

Brian joined Sally as she ran through the details of the case with the rest of her team. They bounced ideas off each other for a productive hour or so.

Joanna was the first to speak. "Why the nineteen-year gap? Could the perp have been released from prison?"

"Possibly," Sally replied. "Can you look into that for me?"

Joanna made a note on her pad. "Of course."

"There's another possibility we need to consider," Jack said, somewhat reluctantly.

Sally got the impression he was still in a mood with her. She smiled, attempting to make peace with him. "Go on, Jack?"

"We've been poking around the past week…"

She tilted her head. *Tell me something I don't know, partner.* "And?" She perched on the desk next to his and folded her arms.

"And, well, what if we've stirred a fire within someone."

"Someone we've questioned already, you mean?"

"He's right," Brian piped up.

"It's not often I'm wrong, mate," Jack responded sternly.

Sally glanced at the ceiling at the testosterone on show, in Jack's case anyway.

"I agree. You could be onto something there, Jack. Our snooping around, or more to the point, asking questions, might have prompted the killer to have resurfaced again. Possibly brought back memories of what it felt like to kill Millie. Or, another scenario I'd like to put forward, what if the murderer was still in the area and he's heard about the investigation being reopened and has come up with a cunning plan to point the finger?"

"By killing another child?" Brian asked, seeming perplexed by the notion.

Sally shrugged. "Why not? It's not as if we're dealing with a mentally stable person, not if they choose to kill an innocent child. Also, the Pickrel case has been featured on TV, don't forget." She crossed the room towards the whiteboard and circled the names of all the witnesses they'd spoken to in the past week, the Pickrels' ex-neighbours et cetera.

Sighing heavily, she turned back to face the team. "So many bloody unanswered questions. It's so annoying."

"Are we definitely linking the crimes?" Brian asked, taking in what was written on the board.

"I think we have to go down that route. Remember we're looking at the same MO here."

Jack grunted. "That could be down to a copycat killer. I'm going to say something now, and hear me out before you leap down my throat." His comment was aimed at Sally. She nodded for him to continue. "It's bugging me why you've circled everyone's name on that board bar one."

Sally studied the board and shook her head. "Nope, not with you, Jack."

"I think I know where he's going. Louie Pickrel," Brian offered.

Jack's nod was slow and deliberate when it came.

Sally was floored by the suggestion but finally relented and circled Louie's name along with the others. "So what now? We haven't got the manpower to put surveillance on all these people. Do we interview them all again? Ask for alibis as to where they were last night?" She shrugged. "I'm at a loss how to approach this one. Brian?"

"Why don't we think about it overnight? Time's getting on, and I need to bring my boss up to date on things."

Sally nodded and then clicked her fingers. "Actually, that might not be a bad idea. We should have the sketch from the artist by the morning. Why don't you drop by about ten, Brian? Things should be a little clearer by then."

"Yep, I'll do that. Thanks for today, Inspector. It was nice meeting you all." He waved and left the room after the team had responded.

"Well, that's our case put to bed for the night. Want to share with us how you guys got on today, Stuart?"

He picked up his notebook and ran through how their day had panned out. "We decided to go to the sausage factory where Lucinda used to work, to have a word with her colleagues. God, have you ever even contemplated how mundane factory work is? I couldn't stand there on a production line for eight hours a day, I'd go loopy."

Sally smiled and motioned for him to get on with things.

"Anyway, we spoke to three ladies. Two were forthcoming with information, and the third was very reluctant at first."

"Any idea why the third lady was reluctant to speak with you?"

"Not really. Although she did tell us that the other two ladies knew Lucinda better than she had."

"Fair enough. And what did you glean from your conversation with these women, Stuart?"

"The first two, Cora and Liz, still seemed really upset by the loss of their friend. Couldn't understand what had gone wrong in her marriage, told us that Lucinda and Roger were a solid partnership."

"Interesting. Is that the impression you got after speaking with the husband when you visited him in prison the other day?" Sally asked.

Stuart glanced at Jordan. "Have to say yes on that one, boss. He didn't come across as a killer to us. I know we have to be wary of being taken in by these prisoners, but even so. I'd put my house on him being innocent."

Sally rested her chin on her half-clenched hand. "So, if he didn't do it, then who did? She was poisoned, do we know with what? Let me see the PM report on this one, Stuart?"

He passed her the file. She flipped it open and flicked through the loose sheets of paper to find the post-mortem report. She scan read it and paused at the 'cause of death' section. *The toxicology tests carried out found large traces of wolfsbane and deadly nightshade in the deceased's blood.* "Not heard of wolfsbane before. Anyone else?"

"I hadn't," Jordan replied, "So I Googled it. Wolfsbane is more commonly known as aconitum. While I'm not a gardener, I asked my dad, and he said he'd heard about the flower, said it was quite popular at one time."

"Interesting, okay. We've all heard of deadly nightshade, right?"

"Yes, I had, but I Googled it all the same. Here's the thing... I discovered that atropine, a drug extracted from the plant, is used in eye examinations."

Sally raised a finger. "I see where this is leading. It's possible that someone was being treated for an eye problem and they used the medication to poison the poor woman."

"You want me to delve into people's medical records?" Stuart asked, wide-eyed.

"I think that's going to be the only way we find out what truly happened to this woman. How many people worked at the factory?"

"We're talking around eighty, boss. That's going to be a lot of research; time consuming."

"Might be worth having a word with the line manager to see if the women remained in one section working alongside the same people or if they were moved around from section to section."

Stuart nodded. "I'll get on that in the morning."

"It might also be worthwhile revisiting the women and questioning them further, see if they can remember anyone having an eye problem at the time. Ask them discreetly, of course."

"Again, we'll kill two birds and revisit the factory, speak to the line manager and the three friends again tomorrow."

"Sounds like a plan, Stuart. Okay, not sure about you guys, but I've had enough for one day. I know it's early, but let's go home, get some rest. I have a feeling once we have the results from the sketch artist it's going to be a case of all hands to the pump."

The team switched off their computers and left. Sally slipped into her office to collect her coat and handbag and emerged to find DCI Green standing in the outer office.

"Hello, sir. You startled me there for a second. Can I help?"

"Working part-time nowadays, Inspector? I don't think that was in your renewed contract. If it was, I don't remember seeing it or signing off on it."

"Sorry, sir. This is a one-off. The team weren't getting anywhere. We've got a few leads to follow up on but we're waiting for the results of the sketch artist to come through before we can tackle anything major. They're turning up early in the morning; they'll make up the time over the coming days, I promise, we always do," she added. *Bloody cheek! How come he never shows up when we're eating a takeaway at our desks at ten o'clock at night? Bloody sod's law can do one!*

"Yes, yes. I've heard on the grapevine that your cold case has overlapped a crime that has just been committed, is that correct?"

"It is, sir. We've been working all day with DS Brian Jessop. There are definite similarities to the Pickrel case, and I decided it would be better to join forces. I'm sorry, I never thought to run it past you first, sir."

"Never mind, mistakes happen, Inspector. Do your best to avoid getting into bother in the future would be my advice." His tone was stern and uncompromising.

"I'll be sure to remember that, sir. Was there anything else?"

"No. Just thought I'd drop by to get an update on your case. I've told you numerous times to keep me in the loop, and yet you're still failing to do that, Inspector Parker."

"Sir, in my defence, if there was anything worth sharing with you, I would have. The investigation has been one fuelled by frustration so far. Hardly worth bothering you with, I promise you."

He grunted and nodded. "I still expect you to keep in regular contact with me."

"Sorry, sir. I will do from now on, even if it's to share my frustration on a case."

He turned on his heel and called over his shoulder, "You do that, Inspector. I want you checking in with me every few days."

"Yes, sir," she replied, giving him the finger as he left the room. *Calm down. He's not worth getting all het up about. It's home time. Tomorrow is another day.* Indeed it was. Sally hoped against hope that all the children in the area would be safe in their beds that night, with a child killer on the loose.

9

Sally's alarm went off at seven the following morning. Sleepily, she slammed her hand on the button to shut the damn thing off, rolled over and flung her arm over Simon. She kissed his naked back. "Morning."

He shifted in the bed to face her, pecking her head as he lifted it to place his arm underneath. "Good morning, darling. Did you sleep well?"

"Surprisingly, yes. Even though my dreams consisted of me chasing a bloody intruder caught in the act of smothering a child in her bed."

"Ugh…not good."

She inhaled a large breath then let it out slowly. "One night I can put up with. Can you imagine how the Pickrels feel, or Louie Pickrel in particular? He must relive that nightmare over and over again."

"The poor man. The death of a child must be the worst thing ever; however, to witness that death and feel useless that you could do nothing to prevent it from happening must be absolutely crushing."

"Agreed. Hopefully we'll be able to give the family the news they've been longing to hear in the near future."

"You seriously think the two cases are connected?"

She sat up and looked down at him, her hand placed on the greying fuzz decorating his chest. "Don't you?"

"I'm prepared to remain open-minded on this one."

"May I ask why?"

"Because of the years between the two crimes. As yet, no evidence has been found at the new scene, not that there was anything found at the original crime scene anyway. Oh, I don't know, to me, something doesn't feel right, and I can't seem to put my finger on what that is. Maybe that's my fault for spending too much time away from the lab."

"Nonsense, your instincts are pretty spot on usually. So what if you're not a hundred percent invested in the case. You're entitled to have time off, Simon."

"I know. I'll get back into the swing of things soon enough."

She kissed him, sensing his love for his career waning more than ever. "If your heart isn't in it any more, love, you need to take a step back and seriously consider your future."

"I've been doing that for a while, just not sure I'm willing to take the final step and give up on all that training."

"It's a decision not to be taken lightly; I know you're not likely to do that. Give me a shout if you need to bend my ear, although the ultimate decision has to be down to you."

"I know. I still have to weigh everything up. I'm fortunate in that I have two successful careers to choose from now. Maybe that's the cause of the dilemma going around my head."

She flung back the quilt and left the bed. "I value our marriage, so I'm going to take a step back while you make up your mind. I know whatever decision you make it'll be the right one for you and ultimately for us."

He smiled at her. "And that's why I love you; your support never fails to amaze me. Other women would be frantic, tearing their hair out, forcing me to hurry up with the decision-making process."

She grinned. "In case you hadn't noticed, dear husband of mine, I'm not, and never will be, like other women. I believe a person has the right to make up their own mind about what's important to them in this life. I'll be here if you need guidance but that's as far as I'm prepared to go. Whichever career you decide on is down to you. I'll be behind you all the way."

"As long as the money rolls in, is that it?" His eyes sparkled as he teased her.

She pointed a finger at him. "I'm going to forget you ever mentioned that."

"Good. It was meant as a joke, not a dig in any way."

"As long as I have the love of a good man, money is immaterial to me. A quick question for you."

He tilted his head, inviting her to go on.

"Any idea where I'm going to find this good man?" She laughed and ducked into the bathroom, narrowly missed by the pillow he'd aimed at her.

"I'll get you for that, Mrs Bracknall—when you're least expecting it, I might add."

"Whatever," she replied, stealing the word she hated the most from her partner.

Sally was still smirking when she arrived at work an hour later.

Pat greeted her with a warm smile from his post behind the reception desk. "Morning, ma'am. Nice to see you looking so cheerful."

"I'm always cheerful, Pat. All quiet overnight?" she asked, bracing herself for the answer.

"As far as I know, yes. That'll be a relief for you, I know."

"It is. See you later." She ran up the stairs to find Jack and Joanna chatting over a cup of coffee. Judging by the fullness of Jack's cup as she passed his desk on her way to the vending machine, he hadn't been there long. "Morning, both. Ready for some hard work today?"

"All primed and ready to go, boss," Joanna stated, pointing at her lit computer screen.

"Always ready for hard work. It never seems to come our way, though," Jack complained. "I hate the mundane side of our job, especially working these damn cold cases. I suppose you'll be going out and conducting further enquiries with Jessop today? When he eventually shows up."

"We'll see how things go, Jack. 'Why the long face?' as the bartender said to the horse sitting at his bar waiting to be served."

"That one is as old as the hills. You need to find better jokes to add to your repertoire."

"It's all I had to hand. Maybe it would be more appropriate if you came to work without wearing a damn scowl now and again and then I wouldn't have to resort to digging deep for a joke to come up with to boost your bloody morale."

He poked his tongue out at her. "Ain't gonna happen anytime in the near future."

Sally shook her head and continued on her journey to the vending machine. She opted to ignore his jibe. She was in a good mood and wasn't about to let him bring her down. Brian Jessop joined them a few minutes later, followed by Stuart and Jordan.

"Grab yourselves a coffee, gents. We'll spend the first twenty minutes going over the plans we briefly mentioned yesterday."

The team gathered around, all with a drink in their hands. "Brian, first thing, I need you to chase up the sketch artist, if you would?"

"Already made a mental note to do that, boss." He sipped his coffee.

Sally's glance slipped to Jack who was quietly mimicking what Jessop had said. She shook her head and rolled her eyes when he caught her staring at him. He had the decency to look ashamed by his conduct. *A grown bloody man in his forties? You could have fooled me.*

"I pondered overnight how to proceed and think we should put the interviews on hold in the Pickrel case until that image comes through. Is everyone agreed on that?"

The team all nodded.

"Makes sense to me," Brian added.

"Stuart, I need you and Jordan to go back to the factory and reinterview the women and the line manager. Maybe you showing up two days on the trot will force someone to cast their minds back and come up with something useful. Still tread carefully until a positive connection shows up."

Both men acquiesced with a brief nod.

"Jack, I want you and Joanna to help Stuart and Jordan with their case for now. There's very little we can do on the Pickrel case until that drawing comes our way."

"You want us to go over the medical files, is that it?" Jack asked.

"Yes, it'll be a start. Maybe you should begin with Mick and Lucinda, see if either of them had any problems with their eyes and go from there."

"That could take days to sort out," he grumbled, eyeing Joanna.

She seemed far more upbeat about things, however, and her smile remained in place.

"It could. I'll hold your hand through the process, Jack," Joanna teased.

His cheeks coloured up as the other male members of the team all jeered and whistled. Sally had to suppress a laugh that was on the verge of erupting.

"That's it then, folks, let's make it a productive day. I'm going to deal with the post in my office, then I'm going to ring the prison, see if Seb Randall has had any contact with the outside world since we paid him a visit."

"You think he might have contacted someone on the outside and instructed them to kill that child?" Jack asked in disbelief.

"I don't know, Jack. I'm just trying to think outside the box, cover every possible angle. It can't hurt, right?"

He shrugged, and she prepared herself for what he was about to say next. "Whatever."

"I'm out of here," she said, walking into her office. She closed the door behind her and sat behind her desk. After looking up the number of the prison, which she should know off by heart by now, she rang Governor Ward.

He sounded pleased to hear from her. "Hello, Inspector. What can I do for you?"

She explained the situation, and he sounded shocked by the news.

"I don't understand. You're suggesting that Randall had something to do with this little girl's murder?"

"The truth is, I don't know, sir. I'm covering all the bases until something concrete comes our way. Do you know if he's had any contact with the outside world?"

"I do and I can categorically say, he hasn't. However, in the circumstances, I will speak to my staff, see if any of them have seen him placing a call within the last forty-eight hours, how's that?"

"Excellent news, I was hoping you'd say that. I'll wait to hear from you then. Thanks again for being so obliging."

"No thanks needed. Speak to you soon, Inspector."

Sally ended the call and sat back, contemplating how feasible it would be for Randall to make such arrangements with the guards watching his every move. She didn't hold out much hope of the governor coming through for her.

She tried to get on with some paperwork while she waited for the governor's call—it proved to be pointless.

Governor Ward rang back twenty minutes later. "DI Sally Parker. How may I help?"

"Inspector, it's me."

"That was quick, Governor. Do you have any news for me?"

"Yes, however, I don't think it's the type of news you've been expecting."

"Don't tell me. Randall hasn't set foot near a telephone in weeks."

"You've got it. Sorry to disappoint you. Good luck with your investigation."

"Thanks for getting back to me so promptly. No doubt our paths will cross again soon in the near future."

"I'll look forward to that."

She could hear the smile in his voice and ended the call. Leaving her paperwork to one side, she returned to let the team know. Brian was no longer in the room.

"Your attention please, folks. I've been on the phone to the prison. We can cross Sebastian Randall off the list of possible suspects. He hasn't made contact with anyone in the outside world in weeks."

"I thought you were chancing your arm with him," Jack replied, folding his arms.

"It needed to be checked all the same, Jack."

Sally had to bite her tongue. His attitude was ticking her off. If she let rip at him now, though, there was no telling what he was likely to do. She needed every available team member on this one. In some ways, she regretted giving Stuart and Jordan the other case to work on. But then, they'd progressed well on it, and she sensed that case would be wound up soon enough, then she'd have the full team at her disposal again to check through the alibis of the other witnesses.

Although, if Jack persisted in acting like a child, she'd be eager to leave the office just to put some distance between them. She walked over to the machine and bought herself a coffee. Brian came barging into the room, waving a sheet of paper, stopping her in her tracks as she was returning to her office.

"We've got it," he shouted excitedly.

"Let me see." Sally rushed to have a look, almost spilling her coffee in her eagerness. "Jack, get the E-FIT from the Pickrel case, will you?"

He grunted and searched the edge of his desk in no great hurry.

Brian handed her the sketch artist's drawing, and Sally gasped. She didn't have to make a comparison. Both pictures were exactly the same. She glanced up at Brian. His enthusiasm had dimmed once he'd studied her expression.

"It's not possible," she muttered.

Jack held out the original E-FIT, and Brian looked at it.

"No way!" Brian murmured in disbelief.

"Are you going to let me and Joanna see that damn picture?" Jack demanded impatiently.

Sally turned the picture to face the two team members, and they had the same reaction she had.

"Bloody hell, that can't be right. There must be some mistake," Jack said, shaking his head.

"It's the genuine article. That's who the neighbour saw," Brian told them. He collapsed into the nearby chair. "What does this mean?"

Sally took both pictures and pinned them side by side on the noticeboard. "I have an interpretation for you, but you're not going to like it."

"Go on," Jack said, "Surprise us."

"Someone is intent on messing with our heads," Sally revealed, her heart sinking as she said the words out loud.

"Seriously?" Brian asked. "Why?"

She shrugged and perched her backside on the nearest desk as she contemplated her response. She failed to come up with anything suitable. "I haven't got a clue."

"Mind games...it's feasible. Or is it? The neighbour gave every detail of the same face that hasn't changed in the nineteen years since the first crime was committed."

"I've got a theory, if you want to hear it," Jack announced churlishly.

"We're all ears, Jack."

"What if the neighbour saw the TV programme the other day and the E-FIT image stuck in his memory and he's gone from that?"

Sally ran a hand over her face. "It's possible. We need to ring the TV station, see if the E-FIT was shown the night the show aired. Jack, can you do that for me?"

"Roger that." He picked up the phone on the desk and placed the call. The answer, when it came, was negative and had them all foxed once more.

"Nearly twenty years, and his features haven't changed. It's inconceivable, isn't it?" Sally asked, shaking her head.

"It is to me. What now?" Brian asked, matching her bewilderment.

"I need to get out of here," she muttered. "Come on, Brian. I wasn't going to do this personally, but the walls are suddenly closing in on me."

Brian's gaze drifted first to Joanna and then to Jack.

"Is there a problem?" Sally snapped.

"No, not at all. Where are we going?" Brian replied.

"To check out the other witnesses' alibis."

He scrambled out of his chair.

She picked up her handbag and returned from her office. "Keep digging, Joanna and Jack, we've got to stumble across something new soon."

"If you say so," Jack mumbled as she walked past his chair.

She slammed a hand down on his desk, startling everyone else, especially Jack. "Cut it out. Give the frigging attitude a rest, for all our sakes, Jack. I've had as much as I can take for one day. Give me a break. Don't you think this case is proving difficult enough without the other crappy stuff you're flinging into the mix?"

"Sorry." He jumped out of his seat and tore his jacket off the back of the chair. "I've had it. I'm not feeling very well. I'm pulling a sickie."

"What? You walk out of this office, and it's the last thing you'll do around here, partner."

"Huh! *Partner*? That's a bloody laugh. When you're in need of my services again in that department, let me know. I might see you tomorrow. There again, I might not." He stormed out of the room before Sally had a second chance to issue him with a warning.

She slumped on the desk and placed her head in her hands, tears pricking her eyes. *What the hell is happening? Why is everything going wrong? And what the hell is eating Jack? Jealousy? Because of Brian?*

"Is this down to me?" Brian asked.

"If it is, it's his problem, not ours. We should head off. Will you be all right here alone, Joanna?"

Joanna nodded and waved her concerns away. "I'll be fine. Not making excuses for him, but I'm sure Jack didn't mean to strike out like that."

"Is there something going on at home that I'm not aware of, Joanna?"

"I don't think so, boss." Her gaze drifted from Sally to Brian.

"So it's pure and simple jealousy, is that it?"

Joanna nodded. "Seems that way to me, boss."

"I expected better of him. Oh well, here we go again. If he wants to leave the team then who am I to try and stand in his way?"

"I'm sorry if my being here has caused any ill-feeling between you all," Brian chipped in.

"Don't you dare apologise, you've done nothing wrong. Jack needs to grow up, that's all. He's responsible for getting himself in a tizzy, no one else."

"It's tough when an outsider joins a team, so I kind of get where he's coming from," Brian added, exhaling a large breath.

"That's his fault, not ours. He's not a junior around here, he has approximately ten years of service under his belt. He needs to grow some balls and lighten up. We should go. We have a lot of ground to cover. We'll keep in touch, Joanna. Ring me if you find out anything useful."

"I will, boss. I hope your quest goes well."

"Thanks." She smiled, showing how much she appreciated the constable's loyalty.

10

During the day, in spite of telling herself to calm down, Sally's frustrations got the better of her. She and Brian spent the next few hours reinterviewing the witnesses, ensuring their alibis matched up, leaving them shaking their heads in despair. "I don't get it," she said, slamming her fist against the steering wheel.

"It's tough. Don't let it get to you. I know the situation with Jack is bound to be playing on your mind, too."

"It's truly not. He's made his bed. I'll deal with him when this case has come to a conclusion. I'll be honest with you, I'm lost. For the first time in years, I haven't got a damn clue where to turn next."

"Would it be worth visiting Anna Pickrel? Not sure what I'm suggesting, it's just a thought."

"And say what? Show her the two E-FITs and muddy the water even more?"

Brian shrugged. "Don't forget what Jack suggested yesterday."

She turned to face him. Frowning, she asked, "Remind me? My head's all over the place right now."

"He told us not to keep Louie out of the equation in regard to getting folks' alibis checked out."

She pondered his statement for a moment and then started the engine. "I still think Jack is wrong, but as we've got nothing else to go on, it's worth a shot. First, I think you're right, we should visit Anna and let her know what's going on. She's only around the corner. We might as well see her while we're on her doorstep."

Sally didn't bother ringing ahead; she took the chance the woman would be at home. If she wasn't then she'd ring her later and bring her up to date on things. As it happened, there were two cars sitting in the drive when Sally brought the car to a halt outside Anna's house.

"Let's get this over with," she said, exiting the car.

Brian opened the gate for her and rang the bell. She fixed a smile in place ready for when the door opened.

Louie appeared a few seconds later. He seemed as surprised to see them as they were to see him.

"Hello, Mr Pickrel, it's just a courtesy call to see your mother. Is she in?"

"She is. Come in. I'll tell her you're here."

"Thanks. By the way, this is Sergeant Brian Jessop. He's a temporary member of my team."

Louie shrugged, as if the news didn't concern him, then he showed them both into the lounge where Anna was sitting, reading a magazine.

"Inspector, although it's nice to see you, it strikes the fear of God into me. Do you have any news about Millie?" Anna asked apprehensively.

"Unfortunately, not at this time. I wanted to drop by and see you as we were in the area. Sorry, this is Sergeant Brian Jessop. He and I are working on a couple of cases together."

"Pleased to meet you. Take a seat both of you."

Sally and Brian sat on the spare couch while Louie stood next to his mother.

"Does this mean you're not working full-time on my daughter's case now?" Anna asked, nervously rubbing her hands together in her lap.

"On the contrary. Since we last met, there has been a further incident."

Anna's brow furrowed. "I'm not with you. What are you saying?"

"We're not sure of the whys or wherefores as the other investigation is in its infancy; however, I need to prepare you for some shocking news."

Anna reached for her son's hand. He sank onto the arm of his mother's easy chair.

"Go on," Anna prompted.

"Recently, we were called out to a scene. Actually, Brian is the investigating officer on this one. Anyway, the victim was a child who had been suffocated in her own home."

Anna gasped. She snatched her hand away from her son's and placed both hands over her face. She rocked back and forth saying the word no, over and over.

After a while, with a lump swelling in her throat, Sally pleaded, "Please, the last thing I wanted to do was cause you any distress."

Anna glanced up, her eyes red raw. "Don't you see? It's our fault." She looked up at her son. "You warned me not to take part in that programme. You were right, Louie. I should've listened to you."

He placed an arm around his mother's shoulder. "Hush now, let the inspector talk, Mum. No recriminations, please. We've had enough of them over the years."

Anna nodded and faced Sally again. "I'm sorry. I should've let you finish. Please, go on."

"It's complicated, Mrs Pickrel. While we're linking the two cases, we have to be cautious about doing that, given the length of time between the two crimes. We've spent the best part of the day reinterviewing all the witnesses we spoke to regarding Millie's case, just in case the killer was amongst them, and have to say all their alibis have checked out so far."

"So, where does that leave you?" Louie asked, his feet shifting a little as if he was trying to suppress his impatience.

"No further forward at the moment. Right now, I'm leaning towards the latest crime possibly being by a copycat killer."

"Because they saw it on the programme I took part in?" Anna asked, her voice quivering with emotion.

"Maybe. The truth is, we just don't know," Sally replied.

She nodded slowly. "Stupid question: how are the parents?"

"Devastated, as you can imagine. They were both in the house asleep when it happened. We did have a spark of good news. One of the neighbours told us he saw a man loitering in the street where the crime took place on the night of the murder. He was able to work with a sketch artist." She reached into her jacket pocket for her phone, stood and crossed the room. Flipping through her recent photos, she showed a shot she'd taken of the two sketches sitting side by side on the whiteboard.

Anna shook her head. "No! It can't be, can it?"

"This is the puzzling part which is driving us to distraction, as you can appreciate. Although the drawings were sketched nineteen years apart, they're virtually the same. That is the man you identified, isn't it, Louie?"

He peered closer at the phone, then responded, "Yes. That's incredible. I'm not surprised you're flummoxed, Inspector. What do you intend doing about it?"

"We're running the necessary checks through the system now. I'm not holding out much hope. The forensics team are doing their best to find some form of clue the killer might have left at the recent scene. I need to check in on them when I return to base. Nothing has shown up so far. Like I said, this case was never going to be easy. Almost twenty years after your daughter's murder, adding the new murder has just made it a thousand times harder to solve. I want to reassure you that we're doing our utmost not to let you down. I'm hoping you can understand our plight and are prepared to give us more time to delve into things further."

"Take all the time you need," Louie said, answering for both of them. "Can we do anything else to assist you?"

"No, not really, but thank you for asking. We'd better get back to it now." She tucked her phone away again and walked towards the door while Brian left his comfy seat.

Louie hugged his mother. "You stay there, Mum, I'll show the officers out."

"Thanks, love. Do your best, Inspector."

"Always, Mrs Pickrel. I hope the next time I see you we'll have the killer banged up in a police cell."

They left the house, and Louie shook their hands at the front door. "Thank you for keeping us updated. Mum didn't say it, but I'm sure she meant to. Can you pass on our condolences to the parents of the little girl who was murdered?"

"I'll be sure to do that. Please, take care of your mother. Hearing this news is bound to bring back memories of what happened to Millie. I wish our visit could've been more positive for you. Hang in there."

"Thank you, Inspector. I'll take care of Mum. We all will."

Sally and Brian returned to the car and set off back to the station. The car journey remained quiet. Had she been alone, Sally would have pulled over into the nearest lay-by and shed a few tears to release the pent-up emotions clawing at her throat and chest. Instead, she was forced to hang on to them.

When they arrived back at the station, Joanna had the TV on and was watching the news. The main story was that of Holly Kilpatrick. The parents were on the screen, arms wrapped around each other, pleading for the public to help the police with their enquiries. Brian looked a bit miffed by the events being shown.

"Everything all right, Brian?" Sally asked. She handed him a coffee she'd bought from the vending machine as she listened to the broadcast.

"Fine. Trust my boss to get in on the act. He's a bit of a control freak. Called me last night to get all the information out of me. Never even mentioned he was going to do a conference about the damn case."

"Ouch! That's got to hurt. Sorry, mate," she replied, rubbing his arm in consolation.

"I know someone who wouldn't treat her colleagues like that," Joanna said quietly.

Sally nodded. "No, I wouldn't. I'm shocked and appalled on your behalf, Brian. Is it my fault?"

"What? Why would it be your fault?" Brian asked, confused.

"If I hadn't suggested you teaming up with us, well, you'd be in the thick of all this." Sally pointed at the screen.

Brian laughed despite his anger. "Nope, you're fine. It's just the way Wagstaff likes to run things. I'll get over it. I have to."

"You're a better person than me, Brian. I'd be absolutely tearing my hair out and ready to beat someone up with a bat if I were in your shoes."

He tilted his head and asked, "You would?"

She pulled a face at him. "Well, maybe I wouldn't be tempted to go that far, but you get my drift. I'm livid on your behalf, how's that?"

"It'll do. Thank you for caring. Truly, it's fine. I guess I have to accept it if I'm going to remain working under Wagstaff."

And if Jack doesn't buck his ideas up, there will be an opening in my department. I'd jump at the chance of having you on board.

"I suppose so, unless another opening comes up for you to transfer to in the near future."

Joanna's head snapped round, and her mouth gaped open. Sally suppressed a giggle and winked at her. The constable shook her head slightly and got back to work.

"I'll be in my office for the foreseeable," she called over her shoulder.

She emerged a few hours later, after raised voices drifted into her office. "What's going on?" she asked Stuart and Jordan.

"Excuse our enthusiasm, boss. We think we've solved the Barratt case."

"You have?" She pulled out a nearby chair and motioned for him to continue. "I'm all ears."

"Well, while I bring you up to date, we'll need you to authorise a warrant, boss, if that's okay? Jordan can sort that out if you're in agreement."

"I trust you. If you believe the evidence is clear, then yes, go ahead and order one, Jordan. Now, get on with it, Stuart, I'm dying to hear how you got on."

Stuart chuckled and pulled out his chair. "As you requested, we went back to the factory and poked around some more. Questioned the three women again who we spoke to previously. Two were obliging, and one was a little reluctant. This stuck out like a sore thumb to both of us. Luckily, we questioned her first and were able to ask the other two women what her problem was." He sipped at his cup of coffee.

Sally patiently waited while he replenished his fluids. "Go on," she asked eagerly.

"Well, one of the women leaned in and whispered, 'You know she's been visiting Mick in prison, don't you?' Well, that statement floored us, as you can imagine."

"Wow, okay. Did they say why or how often this had happened? If it was the once she might've just been offering her condolences."

He shook his head slowly. "The woman said Donna Jarvis, who is divorced by the way, has been a frequent visitor. On the journey back, I got Jordan to ring the prison, and they confirmed that she visits Mick every month. They've been monitoring the relationship, and it has developed into them hugging and holding hands. The prison officers have been forced to intervene on several occasions."

Sally rubbed her chin with her finger and thumb. "Very interesting. No wonder she was reluctant to speak to you. I'm taking it that she worked alongside Lucinda before her death?"

"You presume right. All four women used to be extremely close. Since Lucinda's death, the other two women mentioned they've seen a different side to Donna. From what they told us, they're under the impression that Donna felt awful about Lucinda's death and the fact that Mick is an innocent bystander who is being punished. She told them that she's doing everything she can to keep his spirits up and is hoping to put enough money aside to employ a barrister to take up his case and try to get his conviction overturned."

"I know what you're thinking. Why would she do that unless she knew who the real killer was, am I right?"

Stuart nodded and took another sip of coffee. "Glad we're on the same wavelength, boss. One of the women hinted at a rift between Donna and Lucinda shortly before her death. When I spoke to Donna about it, she averted her eyes and stared at the floor, refused to say anything else. Said she was too upset and didn't want to speak to us any more."

"That's a bit sus in itself, let alone on top of what else you've told me. You're right to ask for a warrant. In the meantime, I think you should pay the husband another visit. Go there and run a few minor things past him and then hit him with why he didn't tell you about Donna's frequent visits. For all we know, they could be in on it together, so tread carefully."

"Shit! I never thought of that, boss. You could be right, otherwise, why wouldn't he have mentioned it to us when we initially questioned him?"

Jordan joined them after he ended his call. "The warrant should be through in the next few days, boss."

"Good, that gives you plenty of time to revisit Barratt and probe him for information about Donna. What you want to get out of him is when their friendship or relationship flourished. In other words, if he and Donna were having an affair while Lucinda was alive. Judge his reaction to that and you'll have your answer if they were in on the murder together or not. The last thing we want to do is set the man free if he's as guilty as sin."

"Got it, boss, although, I have to say, he seems innocent to me," Stuart replied.

"Let's hope you're right. You won't really know until you confront him about Donna's visits. Why didn't he mention that when you visited him? Why the secrecy if he has nothing to hide?"

"True enough. All right if we grab something to eat en route to the prison? We kind of missed out on lunch."

"I'm annoyed you even had to ask me that, Stuart. I trust you guys not to waste time when you leave this office. You're still entitled to eat during the day while on shift."

"Thanks, boss. We'll have our drink and then get on the road again."

"Let me know how you get on with Barratt."

"Will do."

Sally smiled, and her gaze drifted up to the whiteboard. She found herself envying Stuart and Jordan. At least their case was on the brink of being solved, while the Pickrel one was still very much in limbo.

"Penny for them?" Brian asked.

"I just feel as though we're missing something major, and it's bugging the life out of me what that might be."

"If it's any consolation, I'm feeling the same way regarding the Holly Kilpatrick case. Maybe we're guilty of paying too much attention to the artists' drawings."

Sally considered his suggestion for a split second and nodded thoughtfully. "You could be right. However, if we take those out of the equation, we're still up shit creek."

Brian heaved out a frustrated breath and stretched his legs in front of him. "All rather puzzling. If only we had some form of DNA at our disposal. Why? Why and how has the killer been so careful?"

"If we stumble across that any time soon, Brian, I think that'll wrap up the case," Sally replied, narrowing her eyes on the board. The clues were hiding there somewhere. She had a strong feeling about that, but where? All the witnesses had been reinterviewed, their alibis had checked out. There was nothing else for them to do. The latest murder had occurred in a residential area, so there was no CCTV footage available for them to waste time trawling through.

Nothing.

Not even a suspect's car they should be trying to track down.

Nothing.

"We're off now, boss. Do you want us to report back, or shall we go straight home after we've visited the prison?" Stuart asked, slipping on his jacket.

"Depending on the time. If you leave there after six, call it a day and we'll go over things in the morning. Unless you feel up to filling me in on how your visit goes tonight. No pressure on that front from me."

"No problem. We'll get going, and I'll ring you this evening." Stuart and Jordan left the room.

"Waste of time you hanging around here, Brian, why don't you go back to your team?"

Goodbye My Precious child

He rose from his seat and nodded. "I agree. If you're sure. If anything comes in, will you give me a shout?"

"I'll do that. Thanks for your help today. Keep thinking things over. Ring me if anything jars with you, day or night, okay?"

"I will. Be in touch soon, I hope."

Sally watched him leave the room and glanced over at Joanna. "I can see the cogs churning, lady. What's on your mind?"

Joanna leaned back and tapped her pen on her notebook. "I'm concerned about Jack, boss."

She exhaled a breath. "In what way? Has he said something to you that he hasn't bothered to mention to me?" she asked stiffly.

"Not that I'm aware of. Oh God, I hate to say this but…"

"You're going to anyway. Go on, Joanna, I'd rather you air any grievances than let them fester."

"Not a grievance as such, merely an observation, boss. Male pride comes to mind. He's feeling left out of things because you've been out and about with Brian."

She winced. "Really? Is that it, jealousy?"

"Looking at things as an outsider, yes, that's likely the case."

Sally sat forward, placed her elbows on her thighs and rested her chin on her fisted hands. "What is wrong with him? He's aware how much I wanted to be involved in the new case. It was obvious Brian wasn't going to relinquish his hold on it. We're lucky his boss agreed to us working together, he needn't have. As it is, we're still going around in circles."

"I know. You don't have to justify your intentions to me, boss. That's why I placed the scenario under the 'male pride' tab. Men are all mouth until something like this comes along."

Sally sat back again. "It's bollocks, isn't it? We never create when something of this nature happens, do we?"

"We're built differently. I mean up here." Joanna prodded her temple.

"I suppose so. I know Jack has this underlying feeling that he shouldn't be on the team; however, I thought he was past all that crap.

Do you think he's searching for another job, or at least another role at the station?"

Joanna shrugged. "Maybe. That didn't work out too well for him in the past, though."

"Any suggestions how I handle things when he returns?"

Joanna held up her hands. "Whoa, it's not for me to tell you how to deal with your team, boss. Maybe I should've kept quiet about this."

"No way. I appreciate you being so open with me. My dilemma is how to put things right, not that I think I'm in the wrong. Jack's a good man, I'd hate to lose him, but if his heart isn't in it…what can I do to change his mind?"

"Do you want me to have a word with him? I'd willingly do that but didn't want to go ahead and end up stepping on your toes."

"By all means, have a word if you will, if it's not too much hassle for you to contend with."

"It's not. I'll have a quiet chat with him tomorrow. Stick the boot in if I have to. He's a valued part of this team and in my eyes is being downright irrational about Brian working with us right now."

"Thanks, Joanna. You're a treasure. I'm going to deal with the paperwork I've yet to finish. Give me a shout if anything crops up that you feel needs my attention."

"Will do, boss. Actually, I'll give Jack a ring now, see if everything is all right with him."

"Let me know how you get on."

Joanna reported back an hour or so later. It had taken her a little while to get in touch with Jack. He'd taken his granddaughter for a stroll at a nearby park to chill out and was feeling better after his time off.

He assured Joanna that he'd show up for work in the morning and that his mind was clearer now. Sally was relieved to hear the news and drove home feeling confident that everything would be good as far as Jack was concerned in the morning.

She decided to stop off at the supermarket on the way home. She rang Simon during the journey to see if he needed anything for dinner. He said he didn't. She decided to treat them to a tub of Häagen-Dazs ice cream each. It had been a while since she'd consoled herself, sitting in front of the TV, eating a tub of ice cream.

Simon must have been watching out for her as he opened the door before she had the chance to insert her key in the lock. "Hello, you. I've missed you today."

He hugged her tightly and almost took her breath away.

"Enough to want to kill me?" she asked, pulling away and laughing.

He lowered his head and kissed her.

She placed a hand against his cheek.

"I needed that after the day I've had. How has your day been?" he said, linking arms with her and steering her through the large hallway into the kitchen. He beamed and gestured at the large bunch of flowers sitting in a vase in the centre of the table.

"Wow, I'm not sure what I've done to deserve this, but it's much appreciated, love. They're beautiful."

"You're beautiful," he whispered against her ear.

If she hadn't been so hungry, she would have melted into his arms and let him carry her upstairs to bed. "What's for dinner?" She lifted the carrier bag in the air and added, "I bought ice cream."

He laughed. "It puzzles me how the dickens you stay so slim. You're constantly thinking about food."

"I am *not*. Well, maybe, a little," she conceded. "I needed cheering up, and ice cream must be full of good ingredients that help to put a smile on one's face."

"You really want me to list the ingredients and the preservatives they add to each pot? I can assure you, if I did, you'd never be tempted to eat another ice cream again."

"Eww...no. I neeeeeed this, don't spoil it for me."

He laughed, kissed the tip of her nose and went to check on the contents of the oven.

She peered over his shoulder, drawn by the wonderful aroma. "What is it?"

"Moussaka. I wasn't sure if you liked it or not, so I took a punt."

She chewed her bottom lip. "I can't say I've ever tried it. I'm willing to give it a go, it smells divine."

"Good. Do you want a coffee or a glass of wine? I'm guessing the latter."

"You guessed right. I'll pour it. You're always running around after me."

"You're worth running around after. I take it you've had another frustrating day at work?"

"Understatement of the decade. Although, two of my team members are close to solving the other case we have on the go at the moment, which is a huge relief. We've arranged for a warrant to be served. Your guys will probably be called in for assistance within the next few days."

"Excellent news. Ring me when you need our help."

Sally nodded and poured a glass of the red Bordeaux Simon had opened to allow it to breathe, discounting any likelihood that she might have opted for a coffee.

She put her glass down on the table. "How long?"

"You have time to change if that's what you're asking."

"I'll be back in a jiffy. Need to get out of this suit before we eat. I have a feeling my skirt won't fit me after we've demolished that lot."

"If there's too much we can bung it in the freezer," he called after her as she ran up the stairs.

"We'll soon see about that," she shouted back, chuckling. She rarely ever left anything he cooked; he was a superb chef. Over the past year or so, she'd tried her hardest to persuade him to enter *Master-Chef*, but Simon refused to buckle, saying it just wasn't for him. She tore off her suit and replaced it with a pair of black leggings and a pink T-shirt then returned downstairs.

"Will I do?" she asked, twirling on the spot in the kitchen doorway.

"You always look fabulous, no matter what you wear. Although I'd rather have you naked and barefoot all the time."

"I'm so glad you didn't add the word *pregnant* to that."

He roared with laughter and turned his attention to serving up the dinner.

She sat at the table and noticed a large white window envelope beside her place setting. "What's this?"

"The contract. I managed to pull a few strings and pushed it through early."

"The house? Oh my. How early?" Thoughts of spending the next few months packing boxes flashed through her mind.

"Four weeks away. I need to check over the contract thoroughly before I send it back. We could sit down and do that together later, if you're up to it, or would you rather tackle it at the weekend?"

"No, this evening will be fine," she replied, hundreds of butterflies taking flight in her stomach at the same time.

"You seem a little down. Are you worried about the house?"

"No, sorry. I'm more concerned about the work ahead of us, packing all those damn boxes. It's a daunting task on top of everything else."

"No need for you to worry. I'll hire a removal firm and let them deal with it all."

"Really? They'll do all the packing as well?"

"Of course they will."

She shrugged. "Wow, how the other half live. I've never used a firm before. Dad's always hired a van and moved my paltry belongings in the past."

He pinched her cheek. "You're a strange one at times. I don't mean that in a condescending way either. Let's eat and plan what lies ahead of us later."

She wasn't about to argue. In fact, she was happy to have something else other than the Pickrel case occupying her mind for the evening.

11

Earlier than anticipated, the warrant to search Donna Jarvis's house was sitting on Sally's desk the following morning. She called a quick meeting with the team—neither Brian nor Jack were included. She was disappointed that Jack had neglected to show up. He'd rung her on the way into work, sounding as if he was putting on a fake croaky voice. Rather than call him on it, she accepted that he was genuinely ill and told him to get in touch when he was better. Now, effectively she was two team members down, but she didn't let Brian's absence get in the way of what she and the rest of the team had to do.

Stuart had rung her the previous evening and given her the bare bones of how the meeting had gone with Barratt. Now, she insisted he brought the team up to speed on that.

"He told us that Donna had started visiting him not long after his wife's death. At first, he thought she was showing him compassion because she was Donna's friend, but then her demeanour changed, and her visits became more intense. He admits to having fallen for her easier than he should have."

"They're an item? Is that what you're saying?" Joanna asked.

"As much as they can be with prison bars between them. I had a word with one of the officers, and he confirmed that he'd had to separate them on more than one occasion during one of her visits. She was all over him, touching his hand, his face, hugging him when she was ordered not to touch him."

"And what was Mick's reaction?" Sally asked, perplexed.

"The officer said he appeared uncomfortable by her overly zealous behaviour. What I forgot to mention yesterday was that when we spoke to Liz at the factory, I dug a little deeper about the two of them falling out, she told us that Donna and Lucinda had fallen out at the last Christmas party Lucinda attended."

"Did she say what that was over?"

"Apparently, Lucinda caught Donna making eyes at Mick."

Sally nodded. "Did she now? So there's your motive. You definitely think Mick had nothing to do with his wife's death? They weren't in some kind of partnership back then?"

"I didn't get that impression in the slightest, boss. Did you, Jordan?"

"Nope. He seems innocent enough to me," Jordan confirmed.

Sally rose from her seat. "Okay, let's go serve the warrant and bring her in for questioning. Joanna, will you hold the fort? I haven't got a clue if Brian will be joining us today or not."

"I'll ring you if he shows up. Anything in particular you want me to do?"

"Keep going over everyone's background, if you will? Something has to show up soon."

"Hopefully," Joanna replied. "Good luck."

Sally, Jordan and Stuart arrived at the house to find it empty. The neighbour butted her nose in when she heard them breaking down the door to gain access to the property. "'Ere...you can't do that!"

"We can, we have a warrant. Go back inside, there's nothing for you to see here, madam," Sally ordered the concerned, irate neighbour.

The woman scooted back into her house and slammed the front door.

"I'll go upstairs. Stuart, you search downstairs, and Jordan, you go out the back, see if there's a garden shed or some sort of storage out there."

The two men nodded. They all pulled on latex gloves and set off in different directions at the bottom of the stairs. First stop for Sally was the main bedroom. She searched the contents of the chest of drawers and the small piece of furniture that she presumed Donna used as a dressing table. All she found were lots and lots of different brands of makeup and perfumes, enough to fill a whole display cabinet at Debenhams, Sally suspected. She moved on to the bathroom. There was a wet towel lying on the floor beside the bath and an overflowing washing basket in one corner. Apart from that, the pink suite was in need of a good clean, although Sally had to admit she'd seen far worse bathrooms over the years. There was a glass cabinet above the sink. She opened the door and peered inside. Among all the cough mixtures and cold remedies, she discovered a tiny bottle hidden at the back. "Stuart, come up here a sec."

"On my way," he shouted back and thundered up the stairs to join her. "Have you found something?"

"I think so. Eye drops. Whether they'll match up, I'm not sure. They were hidden at the back. Let's pick her up and bring her in for questioning."

Stuart rang the station and organised for uniform to pick Donna up from the factory and take her to the station for questioning with the desk sergeant.

"Okay, our job is done here." She popped the eye drops in an evidence bag and passed it to Stuart to fill in the label. Sally called Simon who was back at work for a few days to explain the situation and to organise for SOCO to come to the house.

They arrived back at the station as a patrol car was entering the car park. A uniformed officer got out of the car and guided the handcuffed Donna Jarvis through the main entrance.

"Want me to question her, boss?" Stuart asked, a hopeful tone to his voice.

Who was she to stand in his way of glory? "Go for it. Jordan, you sit in on the interview as well, will you?"

"Thanks, boss, we both appreciate you having the confidence in us."

Sally shook her head, annoyed Stuart should say such a thing. She pointed a finger at him. "Listen up, if I didn't have confidence in your abilities, neither of you would be on my team, got that?"

Stuart nodded sheepishly. "Aye, reading you loud and clear, boss, sorry. We'd better get in there."

Sally pulled his arm. "Put her in a cell for a few minutes, it usually rattles them. You're going to need to wait for either her solicitor or the duty solicitor to show up before you conduct the interview anyway."

"Damn, okay, I forgot that. I'll have a word with the sergeant, see if he can sort that out for us."

"Be gentle, but don't hold back. I have a feeling that once you show her the evidence found at her house, she'll spill her guts."

Stuart and Jordan joined Sally and Joanna a couple of hours later. They were both beaming, pleased with the outcome of the interview.

"I take it things went well?" Sally asked, leaning back in her chair.

"Yep, once she started, her mouth never stopped moving, and then the floodgates opened. She admitted to adding the eye drops to Lucinda's cups of coffee in the canteen. She was always the one who volunteered to collect the drinks. When she stopped to pick up the sugar and cutlery for their meals, that's when she slipped a few drops in Lucinda's drink. She said she felt guilty when Lucinda died and regretted her actions."

"Ha, easy to say now she's been caught. If she thought that much of Mick, how could she let him be tried for his wife's murder? The logic buried in people's minds astounds me at times. Okay, let's get the case wrapped up. I'll get on to the CPS, tell them what you guys have unearthed and get the ball rolling on Barratt's release. Congratulations both of you, you nailed it." She high-fived them both, delighted for all of them.

"Thanks, boss, it feels good knowing that our work will be setting an innocent man free," Stuart replied.

Sally beamed, content that at least one of their ongoing cases had been solved.

Later that evening, after celebrating with a glass of wine, Simon and Sally were snuggled up on the couch, the TV off, making plans surrounding the move.

"Have you decided what you're going to do with this place yet?"

Simon smiled. "I'm going to keep it. We should achieve a high rent on this one. I won't let it out to just any old Tom, Dick or Harry, though. And no, that's not me being snobby. This place should attract a quality renter."

Sally had her doubts. Had they lived in the heart of London, then yes, she would be inclined to agree with him. This was sleepy Norfolk, not the bustling capital. However, the commute from London appeared to be attracting more and more business people to take a punt on the area.

"You're quiet. What are your thoughts on it?" Simon asked.

Her mobile ringing on the table beside her put an end to their conversation. "It's Brian, I should get this. Do you mind?"

"Go right ahead. Want a top-up?"

"I'd love one." She tapped the button and said, "Brian, hi. You're not still at work, are you?"

"Yep. Umm…I apologise for calling so late, thought you'd want to hear this first-hand."

Something in his tone made her sit up. She placed her hand over her glass, preventing Simon from pouring extra wine in it. "Okay, you've got my attention. What's going on?"

"I was called out to a scene this evening, another attempted break-in…" His voice trailed off.

"Okay, I'm not liking where this is leading. What are you saying? No, don't tell me you've gone and caught the bastard?"

"Yes, boss. Umm...I think you need to come out here and see for yourself."

"Shit! I can't believe it. This is excellent news. I'm heading out the door now. Give me your location."

He gave her the postcode of the address where he was, his tone subdued.

"I should be there in ten minutes. Don't move."

"I won't. We're not going anywhere. Drive carefully." Brian ended the call.

"Oh God, sorry, Simon," she called as she ran towards the car and pressed the key fob. "Duty calls. Brian has arrested a suspect. I have to go. You understand, don't you?"

"Of course. Don't worry about me. Be aware of how much you've drunk tonight. Even one glass can alter your reactions and thinking."

"I'll be fine. Anxious to see who the bastard is. Brian was very cagey and refused to tell me. I'll ring you when I can." She waved and slipped behind the steering wheel.

During the journey, the witnesses' faces ran through her mind. She tried to pluck a guilty name out of the mix but couldn't.

When she arrived, the street was lit up with flashing blue lights. She spotted Brian standing at the end of the road, anxiously pacing the area awaiting her arrival, or so she presumed, unless something had gone drastically wrong.

She parked and shot out of the car. He rushed to meet her.

"Who is it?"

Brian shook his head. "You'll see for yourself soon enough." He held up an evidence bag, the contents of which was a latex mask. "He was wearing this."

Sally shook her head. "Hence the reason the culprit hadn't aged."

They upped their pace and crossed the road to the patrol car. Brian appeared to be intent on getting in her way of viewing the suspect which only heightened her anxiety.

Once they reached the car, Brian yanked open the rear door and motioned for her to peer inside the vehicle.

She gasped and took a step back. "Jesus, you!"

The man grinned back through the bruises and cuts on his face. "You never suspected a thing, did you? I had you fooled from the very first day. Even that Falkirk had no idea. He was such a dickhead, it was easy to fool him."

Sally stared aghast at Louie Pickrel.

She shook her head and turned to Brian. "Bloody hell. Has he hurt anyone?"

"The father caught him entering the child's room. He heard a noise outside the house and dragged Pickrel out of the window as he tried to climb through it. They had a scuffle, the father won. He pinned Pickrel down on the ground and called the neighbour for help. The neighbour rang nine-nine-nine and assisted the father in keeping Pickrel secured. I ordered the father to get checked over at the hospital. He had a few cuts and a suspected broken nose."

"Bloody hell. He's to be admired for hanging on to him. Jesus, what in God's name is Anna going to say?" She glanced back inside the car and witnessed a deranged smile pull Pickrel's lips apart.

"It's been joyful seeing her suffer all these years," he stated in a weird singsong kind of voice.

"That's why you killed your own sister? To put your own mother through hell? What kind of perverse excuse for a human being are you?"

His eyes had turned black, matching the evil twist to his mouth. Looking at him made her skin crawl. How the hell Anna was going to cope when she learned the news deeply concerned her. She was aware she needed to inform the mother right away before the camera crews she'd seen arriving had a chance to set up. "Get him out of here, Brian. This mob will have a bloody field day if they see him."

He slammed the back door of the car shut, allowing them some privacy to speak. "I'll go with them. I've arranged for uniform to take down the statements. Can I leave the mother to you?"

"Sure. I know this is predominantly your case; however, I'd like to be there when you interview him. Would that be okay?"

"I was going to suggest the same thing. If anything, I think you should take the lead during the interview."

She forced out a smile. "Thanks, I appreciate that. I'll drive over to the mother's now and meet you back at the station in an hour or so, providing she doesn't need me to stay with her longer than anticipated. I'll keep you informed. Be careful of this one. Keep the cuffs on him. I wouldn't put it past him to attempt an escape. Although he looks pretty resigned to his fate from where I'm standing."

"I'll watch him and rip him to shreds if he tries anything."

She nodded and returned to her car. She scrolled back on the satnav to locate Anna's address and selected it. Her heart thundered rhythmically against her ribs during the drive. She called Simon once she hit the main road. "I can't talk for long. You'll never guess who the killer was."

"Who? No, wait, let me try. One of the old neighbours?"

"You're so far off the mark with that one. We all were. It was the bloody son all along. Louie Pickrel."

"No way! Seriously? Why?"

"To punish his mother apparently. I'm on my way to see her now and then I'm going back to the station to interview Pickrel. Don't wait up for me."

"What a sick shit. Christ, that's totally unbelievable. Be careful when you question him."

"Don't worry. There will be another officer in the room as well as Brian."

"Good. I'll leave you alone now. See you later."

"Love you, Simon. Thanks for understanding."

"What's there to understand? I know how important your career is to you, and rightly so."

She smiled and blew him a kiss. Several minutes later, she arrived at Anna's house. Her husband opened the door. He was surprised to see her there when she introduced herself, not having met him before. He welcomed her into his home and led her through to the lounge where

Anna was reading a book on the sofa. She peered over her half-rim glasses at Sally and gestured for her to take a seat on the couch.

Sally inhaled and exhaled a few deep breaths, preparing herself for what lay ahead. "Hello, Anna. I have some news for you."

Anna placed her book across the arm of her chair and sat forward, alert and ready for Sally to continue.

Crap! I wish this was down to someone else. I'm about to break this woman's heart in two for the second time in twenty years.

"I'm listening, Inspector. Have you discovered some evidence in Millie's case?"

"No. It's more than that. You're aware of the murder of another little girl the other day?"

Anna nodded. "Yes, you came and informed us about that yourself. Have you caught someone? Is that what you're about to tell me? Please, don't keep me waiting any longer. I've spent the past nineteen years of my life praying that a police officer would utter the words 'we've made an arrest'. If you have, please, tell me now."

Sally nervously ran a hand over her face. "This evening a suspect was apprehended as he tried to break into a house. We fear he was about to kill one of the children inside the property."

She gasped. "Gosh, I'm so glad you caught him before the parents had to go through the same torment I've suffered over the years."

"Who is it?" Malcolm Forbes demanded, his eyes narrowing.

"I'm sorry to have to inform you that your son, Louie, was arrested this evening."

Anna seemed confused for a split second. She recovered quickly to ask, "What? For what? No! You're telling me he's the one who…?"

Sally nodded. She glanced up at Malcolm for assistance. He took the hint and moved the book from the arm of the chair and sat next to his wife to comfort her.

"He did this?" Malcolm whispered, shocked.

Anna swiftly turned to look at him. "No. Not my Louie, he wouldn't have done such a wicked thing. Not him, there must be a mistake."

"There's no mistake. I'm sorry, Anna. He was found at the scene wearing a mask, intent on fooling us. That mask matched the E-FITs we have. We've yet to interview him, but as soon as he was arrested, he admitted that he'd killed his sister."

Tears streamed down Anna's face, and her shoulders shook as she sobbed out one word, "Why?"

"All I can tell you at this stage is what he's told me so far. He said he wanted to punish you. Do you have any idea what he meant by that, Anna?"

Her breath caught in her throat, and she shook her head slowly.

Malcolm threw an arm around his wife's shoulders and hugged her to him. "Hush now. None of this is your fault. He's lashing out because he was caught, love." He glanced at Sally. "How sure are you that you've caught the right man?"

"One hundred percent sure. I came here to tell you the second he admitted it to me."

"Oh God. What about our son, Callum? Do you think he was intending to hurt him?" Malcolm asked, a terrified expression chasing the concern away from his features.

Anna shrugged and asked, "What about Natalie? Does she know?" She snatched a tissue from the box on the coffee table and dabbed at her eyes.

"Not yet. I came straight here."

Malcolm shook his head continuously as the news sank in. "That poor woman. She was oblivious to the fact she was sharing her bed with a murderer. What about the child? He told us he was going to call her Millie, if it was a girl. What a sick shit! Sorry, love, I know he's your son, but bloody hell, he must be warped to even consider doing that."

"He's no son of mine, not if he's guilty of killing my beautiful daughter. There's no way back from this. I was mortified when I heard he and Natalie intended to call the baby Millie. I didn't say anything to them, though. Maybe I was wrong not to do that. The bastard would have intentionally prolonged my punishment for years to come."

"Christ, how could he do that to you? Hearing her name every day. Seeing the child, knowing there was a possibility it might resemble

Millie. Like I said, he's warped, and I'm glad you caught him, Inspector," Malcolm said, his voice catching a little.

"I'm sorry it's come as such a shock to both of you. I wanted to come and inform you myself at the earliest convenience. I'd better go now. My partner and I will be working late into the night so we can interview him ASAP."

Malcolm squeezed Anna's shoulders and left the arm of the chair.

Anna stared up at Sally and held out her hand. "Thank you. It might've taken the police nineteen years to have solved this mystery, but I knew, the first time I met you that you'd be the one to get to the truth."

Sally shook the woman's hand and did her hardest to hold back the tears threatening to fall. "I'm glad we got to the truth. Sorry it's not the outcome either of us was expecting."

"I hope they throw away the key for what he's put me through over the years. I'll force myself to see him one last time, in court. I want to see his face when the judge announces his sentence."

"That'll be a few months ahead of us yet. I'll keep in touch, Anna."

She nodded, and Malcolm showed her to the front door.

"Take care of her. She's too calm right now. The raw emotions will strike when the news sinks in properly," Sally warned.

12

Sally was exhausted. It was gone four in the morning, and Louie was intent on stringing the interview out.

He was a different man to the one she'd first met. His answers when they came were concise, measured and deliberate.

She asked the same questions for the umpteenth time. "Why? Was it envy, Louie? Were you jealous of the way your sister was treated?"

His gaze remained on her, a sneer etched into his features. Still he refused to answer the question.

"Your mother was under the impression that you loved your sister. Was it all a ruse? A sham? Were you biding your time? Had you always despised your sister? When did it first occur to you that you wanted to kill her?"

A grin developed on his evil face. His eyes boring into hers, he said proudly, "I knew the day she was born that she wouldn't make old bones."

"How could an innocent child cause so many damaging feelings?"

He shrugged.

"Does Natalie know? Have you ever confided in her?"

"Nope. She's as much in the dark as the rest of you."

"What would have happened to the child you're expecting?"

His grin broadened. "If it's a girl, she'll be called Millie, to prolong my mother's pain, and if it's a boy, I would teach him everything I know."

Her interest piqued. "Meaning what? How to kill?"

"Everything I know, Inspector," he repeated.

Sally swallowed. *What is he telling me, that Millie and Holly aren't the only children he's killed over the years? Are there more bodies out there? Other murders that remain unsolved?* "There are others, aren't there?"

His gaze became more intense, and a sparkle appeared in his black eyes.

"How many are we talking about? In this area?"

He glanced down at the table and then back up at her. He held up his hands. The only digit not extended was his right thumb.

"Nine others? Is that what you're telling me?"

He nodded.

"For the recording, Mr Pickrel is nodding. Where?"

He smiled. "I've been a travelling salesman for years."

Shit! I forgot all about that. The possibilities could be endless. How can I trust what he says? It might turn out to be yet another one of his mind games. Damn, you bastard!

"Going back to the night Millie was killed, what if the babysitter hadn't been called away that evening? Would Millie have survived?"

"It was only a matter of time. If the opportunity had failed to present itself that night, then another chance would have come my way soon enough. The bitch was on heat…"

"The bitch? You're referring to your mother?"

"Of course. Bitches on heat end up sprouting more sprogs. She struggled to cope with the two she was raising. There's no way she could've managed looking after another one."

"Your mother did her best for you. She was entitled to go out and have a life of her own occasionally."

"As long as she didn't spread her legs. That was her downfall. Every time she met a man, she spread her legs and ended up pregnant."

Sally didn't respond. He was clearly delusional. As far as she could remember, Anna had gone out on a date the first time that night in possibly five years. There is no way she was willing to consider her as bad as some of the women she'd come across in her career. He was striking out, doing his best to make Anna look bad in everyone else's eyes as well as his own.

"Why punish your mother when all she did was care for you kids?"

"To teach her a lesson."

"A lesson?"

"She should have stuck with our father. Instead, I had to share my home with two needy women. I had to become the man of the house."

"Ah, I understand now. You were rebelling because your childhood passed you by, that's the real reason, isn't it?"

"I wanted her to go through the turmoil of reliving that night for the rest of her life. She shouldn't have been so selfish, going out on a date like that when she should've been caring for her children. What type of mother does that?"

"We're going round and round in circles here. I'm going to bring this interview to an end. We'll get some rest and begin again later."

"If that's what you want, Inspector. If I feel like speaking to you later."

Sally shrugged. "We have your confession. You'll be charged anyway." She motioned for the constable to escort Pickrel from the room and then addressed the duty solicitor present.

"He's a serial killer, I have no doubts about that."

The solicitor, Miss Vaughan, inserted her legal pad in her briefcase. "Seems that way to me. You have to find the evidence to back up that claim, Inspector."

"I have him nailed on two murders. I'll do everything in my power to find the rest of his victims."

EPILOGUE

"You look shattered, Sal, come in."

She hugged Lorne, and they joined Tony in the kitchen which was still littered with dozens of boxes. Sally raised her hand. "Don't say it. I don't care if the place is a mess. I have all this to look forward to in a few weeks."

"Nice to see you, Sal. I'll make a coffee. You two grab a seat," Tony replied.

"Will you be taking time off for the move?" Lorne asked, reaching for Sally's hand and holding it tight.

Sally smiled at her. "No. Simon has it all in hand. A removal firm is coming in. They'll be with us a couple of days, packing up our stuff and then moving it to the other house. That's usually where things end, but Simon has agreed to pay them extra on top so they'll sort the new house out for us at the other end."

Lorne let out a whistle. "Wow, I guess it really does pay to have money then."

"I wouldn't know," she replied, feeling embarrassed by her good fortune rather than her sudden wealth which she really didn't consider was hers. "Anyway, I needed to take a breather from work and was hoping I could run something past you."

"I'm all ears. You know I'll help out if I can. What's up?"

Tony joined them and distributed the mugs. "Want me to stay or to bugger off?"

Sally smiled up at him. "Please stay. I know anything I say to you and Lorne won't go any further."

"You've got that right." Tony smiled, reassuring her.

She exhaled an exhausted breath. She'd spent the past few days questioning Louie Pickrel. Some hours had been excruciatingly boring, as if he was intent on stringing things out on purpose, while dotted in between were hours where he couldn't say enough. It was clearly all a game to him. Sally had been forced to keep an even temper throughout, not to get drawn into his futile mind games.

Sally explained how the interview with the accused had gone. Both Lorne and Tony listened intently, not uttering a word until Sally stopped and asked for their opinion. "Given what I've just told you, what do you think? He's one for mind games, I'm aware of that. Do you think he's toying with me or do you think I should take seriously what he said about the other nine bodies?"

Lorne shook her head and sipped at her coffee. "While I can understand your dilemma, I'd be inclined to believe him. Nevertheless, that will surely open up a can of worms for you. How long has he been a travelling salesman?"

"Around thirteen years, since he was almost nineteen. My thinking is that if he can sink to the depths of killing his own sister then he's not going to think twice about killing anyone else, is he?"

"There is that; however, in his sister's case, well, that sounds like it was exceptional circumstances, in that he set out to punish his own mother. What motive would he have for killing all the others?"

"Except to satisfy the thrill it gave him," Tony piped up.

"True enough," Lorne replied. "Damn, I'm afraid I really wouldn't know how to proceed if something like this fell into my lap, Sal. Morally, I guess I'd want to sink my teeth into it; however, you have enough on your damn plate as it is, dealing with Falkirk's screw-ups."

"I know." Sally pulled a lock of her hair and flinched. "Unless…"

Lorne narrowed her eyes and glanced at Tony then back at Sally. "Unless?"

"Maybe we could all do it, you know, in our spare time. At the end of the day, those families deserve to find out the truth about what happened to their loved ones. Would you guys be willing to work with me on this?"

"Can we discuss it and get back to you? After all, we're both supposed to be retired nowadays."

"Take all the time you need. Give me an answer by the end of the week?" Sally grinned.

"Gee, two days to contemplate things. Okay, we'll get in touch soon."

Sally raised her mug and encouraged Lorne and Tony to do the same. "No pressure. It's still fabulous to have you here in Norfolk, living next door to us. To neighbours and what lies ahead of us, whatever that may be."

"To wonderful neighbours and the adventures ahead of us," Lorne replied, giving Tony a knowing look.

He rolled his eyes and said, "To neighbours and the trials and tribulations ahead of us."

THE END

NOTE TO THE READER

Dear reader,

I hope you enjoyed the latest instalment in the Sally Parker series, Sally and Lorne have a lot of work on their hands in the next novel. You can grab a copy of **The Missing Wife** now.

Or why not try one of my other thriller series?

The first book in the DI Sam Cobbs detective series which is set in the beautiful Lake District is now available for pre-order, pick up your copy of To Die For here.

Maybe you'd also like to try one of my edge-of-your-seat thriller series. Grab the first book in the bestselling Justice here, CRUEL JUSTICE

Or the first book in the spin-off Justice Again series, **Gone in Seconds.**

Perhaps you'd prefer to try one of my other police procedural series, the DI Kayli Bright series here, **The Missing Children.**

NOTE TO THE READER

Or maybe you'd enjoy the DI Sally Parker series set in Norfolk, UK. **WRONG PLACE.**

Also, why not try my super successful, police procedural series set in Hereford. Find the first book in the DI Sara Ramsey series here. **No Right To Kill.**

The first book in the gritty HERO series can be found here. **TORN APART**

Or why not try my first psychological thriller here. **I Know The Truth**

KEEP IN TOUCH WITH THE AUTHOR:

Pick up a FREE novella by signing up to my newsletter today.
https://BookHip.com/WBRTGW

BookBub
www.bookbub.com/authors/m-a-comley

Blog
http://melcomley.blogspot.com

Join my special Facebook group to take part in monthly giveaways.

Readers' Group